THE PHANTOM ENFORCER

FIRST RESPONDER SERIES
BOOK TWO

J.W. JARVIS

Big Dee Books

JOIN MY VIP READER CLUB

J.W. Jarvis' VIP Reader Club members get free books, access to discounts, and other unique items to accompany the books.

Members are always the first to hear about J.W. Jarvis' new books and publications.

If you haven't read **Book 1** in the **First Responder Series, The Phantom Firefighter**, there are details in the back of the book on how to get it for **FREE** by signing up for my **VIP Reader Club**.

The Phantom Enforcer

by

J.W. Jarvis

Copyright © 2023 by J.W. Jarvis

Published by Big Dee Books

This is a work of fiction. Names, characters, business, places, events, and incidents in this book are purely fictional and any resemblance to actual person, living or dead, is coincidental.

Real heroes don't wear capes. For all our First Responders who protect and serve our communities.

EMMY HERNANDEZ

Emmy's granddad was a commander in the Mexican Federal Police. And her dad was a sergeant in the Windy City police force. Her dad could have reached one of the highest positions, chief of police, if he wanted to. He served 15 years in law enforcement. He stayed a sergeant because he always wanted to stay near the action on the streets. Emmy respected that about him. She knew that took a lot of guts and grit. Policing was in her blood, and she had never wanted to do anything else. She felt responsible for maintaining law and order even at a young age.

She remembers being the first one to rush over to break up fights at school, even if it meant potentially getting hurt. In eighth grade, she intervened between two boys fighting over another girl. The first boy, Thomas, passed a note to this girl in history class right before lunch. The second boy, Clyde, saw it happen and decided to confront Thomas in the schoolyard. Clyde thought he was dating the girl because they had exchanged memes, pictures, and jokes over FastGram, a popular social media platform. They had been doing that for about a month, which he thought earned him the right to be her boyfriend. Thomas knew about this but didn't see them hanging out outside their social media circle. He thought the girl was fair game. The conversation between Thomas and Clyde got heated, and a fistfight started. Emmy was talking with a friend at the time but had noticed the commotion out of the corner of her eye. She was very observant. She ran over and got in between the two boys just as Clyde, twice her size, threw a left hook at Thomas. The good news was she stopped the fight but as a result, she spent the rest of the school day with the school nurse.

Noah saw Dani toss the blue book across his room as she shrieked and cursed the book. She gripped the middle finger of her right hand and grimaced in agony.

"What happened?" Noah said as he jerked away, almost falling off the bed reacting to Dani's outburst. He saw a large bead of dark red blood appear on her finger.

"The book pricked me!"

Noah barely had time to respond, "Huh, what do you ...". Noah and Dani connected eyes as paranoia set in while they heard "Plasmador" whispered in their ears.

Not again, Noah thought, as he felt his body tingle while he entered a new physical location. *We were so careful!* Noah did not hear those words, but he also had this weird feeling he did not think them either. He shadowed a woman who looked to be in her early twenties as she was riding in the passenger seat. A plexiglass barrier was in front of Noah. He soon realized he was in the back of the patrol car like he was a suspect.

I'm a police officer now. There it was again.

"I can hear her thoughts," Noah whispered as he looked down to confirm he had no physical body and realized that there were two police officers in the front seats.

Dani turned around and looked fearful as she appeared to stare into the back seat.

You can? And I can see you now, she thought.

"Can we stop at this gas station? I need to use the restroom." Dani asked the driver.

"Sure, partner, I could use some caffeine anyways, feeling a bit worn down, " the officer driving the car replied.

When they parked at the station, Dani exited the car and headed toward the side of the building. Noah felt a strong pull on his phantom body. "Meet you in 10 minutes, Hernandez," her partner yelled as he pulled open the mini-mart's front door. Dani waved in agreement.

Noah was overjoyed not to have a body this time as he had anxiety entering restrooms at gas stations. From experience, they were always nasty smelling, dim and dirty. He had terrible experiences during some trips with his dad, one of which included a spider the size of his fist. He was glad he couldn't touch anything as Dani entered the women's restroom. Surprisingly, this one was not too bad, and he briefly wondered if it was just men's restrooms that were gross.

"Noah, tell me that is you," Dani asked as she locked the door behind her.

"It is, and you are a police officer!"

"Was it the blue uniform, big belt, or holstered gun that gave it away?" Dani joked.

"I just can't believe we are back in Bookland. We were so careful."

"Apparently not; I think a book fiber punctured my finger right through the baseball glove you gave me." Dani looked at her finger and noticed nothing. "... thankfully, the pain is gone."

"So bizarre!" said Noah as he quickly remembered he could still smell when he was a phantom and immediately

4

picked up on the automatic air freshener in the corner of the bathroom that had just sprayed. It smelled like a combination of decaying flowers and heavy cleaning products. He hoped the automated timer wouldn't go off again while they were still there.

"I'm super confused now. Last time, we both possessed bodies, and there didn't seem to be a phantom. Now there is, and I can see it; I mean ... you!"

"I don't get it either. As a firefighter, I was able to hear the phantom but never saw it. My dad also confirmed I couldn't see him when he was a phantom."

Dani thought for a moment. "... and you can hear my thoughts? You weren't able to do that before, right?"

"No, I couldn't. Hey, what do I look like by the way?"

"See for yourself." She pointed to the mirror above the sink behind Noah.

Noah turned to the mirror with a large crack in the middle like someone had hit it and water stains all over the bottom. The bathroom lighting was mainly from the small window above the stall, but enough to see an apparition staring back at him. He probably would have peed in his pants if he had seen himself in the dark. The daylight helped lessen the creepy factor, but it still was eerie. The form was primarily grey and human-like, but his body moved with a slow-motion smoke-like trail. He raised his arm, which happened in real-time, but then the shape of his arm from its previous position would trail

5

behind till it caught up with subtle hints of silver, purple, and white smoky colors. The most distinctive feature was his shiny silver eyes that had no pupils.

"We need to get going," Dani insisted, as she didn't want her partner to worry.

"Gladly, I've seen enough of myself. Open the door 'cause I can't." Noah stated.

"Wait, I better go pee. Close your eyes."

"I don't think I can," Noah responded.

It was a small one-person bathroom, so there was no stall. Dani sat down to do her thing.

If the phantom could turn beat red, it would, but it couldn't. Noah quickly turned away. "Please ... no ... I have never been in a restroom with a girl, not to mention you're a woman ... la la la la ...," Noah made noises so he didn't hear her peeing.

"All done, that wasn't so bad," as Dani moved to the sink to wash her hands.

Noah sighed, "Let's just figure out how to get back to my bedroom, pronto!"

Emmy was still kind of new to the Chicago Police Department being her second year. Being a rookie in the country's second-largest police force was not for the faint-hearted. The six-month academy training was excellent, but using a police tactic you learned in real life can be a real wake-up call. Your senses are much more elevated, as well as your stress levels. The veteran officers also wasted no time making new rookies feel right at home, especially with hazing. It was all in jest, but it's unnerving when you arrive at the station with plenty of time to get in uniform before roll call, and your locker is taped completely shut. You are then late to roll call, where the sergeant questions your loyalty, judgment, and respect for everyone else's time in front of your peers. Dani felt embarrassed just remembering Emmy's experience. Magically, the hazing stopped as soon as the new rookie class arrived at the department. Emmy remembers that day distinctly.

Whenever the workday feels hard, Emmy always thinks about her dad. He persevered as an officer for over 15 years on the dangerous streets of the inner city, receiving multiple honors and awards. It angered her that a microscopic virus from the global pandemic got him. He contracted the virus before vaccines were available, and his body succumbed to it. He passed away before Emmy passed her training academy, which was even more upsetting to her. It was a proud moment for her, and she wanted her dad to see it.

Emmy's mom and dad were the first in their respective families to leave Mexico and move to the States. Her dad was already a police officer in their native country and had to take the training all over again to become one in Chicago. Her mom opened a small flower business and they both eventually got their citizenship. Emmy was born in a suburb of Chicago but was lucky enough to visit her parents' homeland a few times. She couldn't wait to save enough money for a trip to go back and show her granddad what she accomplished.

Dani still couldn't get over the fact that the phantom could now hear her thoughts, which were also Emmy's thoughts. This made the book trip much different, and she secretly hoped Noah wouldn't have any negative thoughts about her. How do you stop thinking when you know someone is listening? She wondered if Noah could relate to Emmy's plight with her father as the pandemic radically changed another person's life. For her friend's sake, she immediately wondered if tonight was one of his scheduled video calls with this mother. Who knows how long they would be stuck in this story. Dani wanted Noah to keep a relationship with his mother, even if she was two states away, and she knew he was looking forward to a trip his mother promised him to visit her in Arizona after New Year.

"So, you went into the convenience store and didn't get me anything? What kind of partner are you?" asked Dani as their police vehicle entered the highway's on-ramp.

Officer Jim Jones was about a foot taller than Officer Emmy Hernandez, and while he was pretty muscular, you could tell he loved to eat. This added some layers of fat where he didn't want them, causing his police uniform to stretch to its full potential. His height and weight gave him a formidable look to any wrongdoers, but only Emmy would have a chance of catching them if they ran. "You didn't say you wanted anything."

"Well, the polite thing would be to ask anyway."

"Have I not been a good Field Training Officer for you? Showing you the ropes over the last 14 months."

Dani hesitated, trying to understand where he was going. "Sure. Are you still looking for kudos for helping me with that traffic stop two weeks ago?"

"Well, now that you mention it ... you're lucky I didn't write you up. So cut the sarcasm, yeah?"

"Or what? Are you gonna complain to your girlfriend? Oh, that's right, you don't have one."

Jim made a sad face, "That was low, Hernandez. You know it's tough with my overtime schedule to meet quality women."

"Don't be a big baby; maybe you should stop looking online for one and go to church or something."

Jim laughed and smiled widely, "You know, I already have one mother."

Just then, the police scanner clicked an alert, *211 in*

progress at the mini-mart at Halsted and 65th Street, proceed with caution.

"Crap, we were just there!" exclaimed Officer Jones, leaving the last part of his mini-mart hot dog hanging outside his mouth so he could grab the wheel with both hands to turn the vehicle around quickly.

Dani grabbed the radio, "10-4, we are en route."

TWO

FAMILIAR FACE

Officer Jones was speeding down the four-lane highway much faster than the posted limit, but for a good reason. They were in an SUV, but the engine had been modified for pursuit. Noah had never seen a speedometer needle go that high before. His mom used to have a sports sedan, and he remembers wondering if it could reach the 140 miles per hour (mph) that was showing as the upper limit on the dashboard. He saw her hit close to 90 before but then realized she was going too fast and, instead of apologizing, used it as an opportunity to remind Noah never to go more than five mph over the speed limit when he can drive. He remembers thinking at the time *Practice what you preach, Mom!* but was wise enough to keep his mouth shut. The police SUV had blue strobe lights on every side of the vehicle. It was incredible how all the cars and trucks just pulled over and out of the way as soon as they saw the lights or heard the sirens. Even with the windows closed, the sirens were pretty loud. *Need to impress the boss,* Noah heard Dani's thoughts as if they were his own as they raced back to the mini-mart, where the two of them had visited the restroom. He started learning more about the rules of engagement at a robbery site from her thoughts, like how sometimes you just had to improvise based on the current situation. Dani wanted Officer Jones, responsible for her field training, to put in a good report at the station once this was over.

"Don't worry, you'll do fine," Noah said, trying to encourage Dani.

What are you doing? Just because I can hear you without whispering doesn't mean others can't. Dani was careful only to think the words because if she said them out loud, her partner would hear her.

"You mean Jumbo Jones here?" Noah sneered.

"Noah, stop!"

"Who's Noah?" replied Officer Jones.

"Huh?" said Dani, realizing she accidentally spoke the words. She quickly thought of an excuse. "Sorry, this road is where my friend Noah crashed his car while I was in the passenger seat as a teenager. It brought back some bad memories."

"Okay, but just know I need to concentrate here at the speed we're going. If you yell out, *Stop!* I'll think I have to take evasive actions to dodge something.

"Sorry, partner. Do you think this guy was casing the joint while we were there?" Casing in criminology is what burglars do to pick their targets. They will survey and watch a place for a period of time before making their moves to ensure they attempt the robbery at the least risky time.

"I hope not; that would mean we weren't very good at our jobs for not noticing him. What makes you think it was a man and not a woman?" replied Officer Jones.

"Seriously? I just left the academy a year ago, and we studied these things. Females only account for about 15% of the criminals arrested for robberies. I think it's a pretty good chance this one is male." Dani replied with confidence.

At almost the same time, Officer Jones and Noah responded, "Nerd alert!" Dani laughed out loud, but it wasn't at what they said as much as their unison response. Noah secretly loved how the officer whom Dani possessed was just as witty as she was.

~

They turned off the sirens as they drove within 100 yards of the mini-mart gas station. Noah observed each of the officers' necks becoming clammy with sweat. Noah could only imagine that no matter how often you face danger, there is always fear. Fear of the unknown becomes anxiety. Anxiety becomes a strength because it keeps you mentally sharp and alert for the unexpected. They parked on the street to approach without warning. Exiting the vehicle, they drew their weapons. As they started to walk toward the entrance, they realized no other cars were visiting the station. Noah was happy that civilians were not around. The air was quiet except for the sound of leaves scraping against the concrete as the wind blew them away from the nearby trees.

Officer Jones pointed to the side of the building. "I got the back entrance. Cover the front." Dani nodded in agreement as she moved cautiously to the double glass door. As Officer Jones disappeared behind the building, a slender figure dressed in all black burst out of the front entrance. In one hand, he was carrying a full, plastic grocery bag, and in the other, a shiny, silver revolver. He used the revolver hand to quickly pull off his black ski mask as he pivoted right.

Noah heard the click as Dani instinctively pulled the hammer back on her 9mm.

"Stop! You are under arrest!"

The robber was startled as he glanced over quickly at Officer Hernandez, then sprinted off.

"Crap!" Dani ran toward him and used her shoulder radio to alert her partner and Dispatch. "He's making a run for it, in pursuit; check on store attendant. The suspect is armed, over."

"Copy that, Officer Hernandez. Officer Jones, confirm the status and if an ambulance is needed," replied Dispatch.

It was nearly dark outside when the chase started, and the absence of lighting in the Englewood neighborhood would make it difficult. That is probably one of the reasons this mini-mart was targeted. The suspect was slender and especially fast as he ran down the sidewalk from the inter-section. Noah felt like his phantom form was attached with an imaginary string to Dani as she bolted after the suspect. He couldn't believe how quickly her new legs were taking the both of them. Just then, a memory flashed in his head of Emmy winning the regional track championship event for the 400 meter dash as a sophomore in high school. Just as she started closing the gap between herself and the suspect, the suspect darted into a nearby dark alley. The alley was not only dark but was also lined with black commercial trash containers. It took some juking skills to avoid running into them due to the low visibility and the speeds at which they were both going.

"Stop!" Dani yelled again, and the suspect looked back to see how close she was. At that moment, Dani experienced a feeling like when you've met someone before, but you can't remember their name. Noah realized that Dani's thoughts meant she might know the perpetrator, and if that were true, he knew it would drive Dani nuts. Seconds later, Noah saw the robber glance back to check on his gain on Dani. An older woman was trying her best to lift a garbage bag into one of the containers just ahead of the suspect. He didn't notice her because his head was turned, causing him to run straight into her at full speed. Noah watched in horror as the woman's frail body was launched 10 feet in front of the suspect. The suspect stumbled but immediately got up and started running again. Dani had to stop and check on the woman.

"Ma'am, are you hurt?" Dani could barely get the words out as she was almost out of breath.

"My hip ... my hip!" The woman squirmed in agonizing pain, laying on the asphalt.

"Dispatch, I need an ambulance at my location immediately. The suspect fled after running into a civilian," Dani looked down at the woman, "Paramedics are on the way."

Noah was amazed at how brave Dani was. This suddenly got so real, and his adrenaline was spiking just like when he was a firefighter. It was amazing how fast Officer Hernandez ran, and he followed behind her just as fast. As a phantom, he didn't tire like she did. The other fantastic thing he couldn't wait to tell Dani when she wasn't preoccupied was that he could see in the dark. He could hear Dani's thoughts as she ran down the alley and how she wished it wasn't so dark. He could see everything, similar to the videos he had seen of the military using night-vision goggles; only everything had a purplish hue instead of green.

Officer Hernandez rendezvoused with her partner after ensuring the woman was safely taken away by the ambulance. The corner lot was filled with police vehicles, an ambulance, and a fire truck as a precaution due to the gas fuel pumps. As the phantom duo entered the mini-mart, the paramedics cared for the store attendant sitting in the corner. Noah was happy to see him alive, especially since this was now an armed robbery. Dani's partner was talking to the store owner near the refrigeration section.

"Officer Hernandez, this is Sajim, the owner," Jim stated.

"Sorry this happened, sir. Have the detectives taken your statement?"

"Yes, did you get a look at the suspect? Our cameras here show he was wearing a mask until he left," Sajim asked.

"I did and will be adding that to our report." Noah wondered why his friend did not mention that she thought she knew the man. "Glad to see your employee wasn't hurt."

"He did a great job; he tripped the alarm, which sent me a text, and that's when I called the police."

"Sir, you should probably hook that alarm into a monitoring system. That way, our Dispatch can be informed right away."

"I know; I just installed this new system and hadn't had a chance to do that yet."

"What's the damage?"

"He took the register till, which had about $400, a roll of scratch-off lottery tickets, and the money in the safe. My attendant opened it for him at gunpoint after the suspect slapped him across the face."

"How much was in there?"

"Well, I empty it every other day, but it had over $2000 in it tonight."

"You should probably empty it daily; this isn't the safest of neighborhoods," Dani advised.

The officers gave their statements to the detectives while their memory was fresh and returned to their vehicle to finish their shift. They were on what is called the second watch for the department. This means their shift was from 12 p.m. to 9 p.m. To cover the whole day, each department had three work shifts. Lately, though, because of the shortages in personnel and the rise in crime, many city police officers have had to work significant amounts of overtime. This resulted in very long days, but the upside was a fatter paycheck, especially since anything over eight hours was paid at 1.5 times their hourly rate. Emmy was saving for a much-needed vacation and didn't mind the extra hours.

"That poor woman, at the wrong place at the wrong time." Jim sighed as he started the vehicle.

"I almost had him, and now I want to catch him even more!" Dani exclaimed.

"You're fast, so that perp must have been in track too when he was younger."

"He was a fast runner, but the darkness definitely didn't help. When I saw his face, I think I recognized him."

"What? Why on earth didn't you tell the detective that?" exclaimed Jim.

"Because I am trying to remember where I recognize him from."

"Unacceptable, Hernandez; you should've been honest with your statement. I'll ask Dispatch to get a sketch artist to come to the station."

"I was planning on putting that in our report, but it is bugging the bejesus out of me because now I can't even remember his features. I thought he was going to shoot me."

Noah leaned close to Dani's air and whispered, "I can help with that."

You can, she thought, *how?*

"Remember, I can hear your thoughts, and this apparition I am in seems to be able to recall it like I was videoing it. I can describe him perfectly to you."

Dani grinned widely. "Why are you smiling?" asked Officer Jones.

"Because I think I just figured out how to remember."

When they arrived at the station, the lieutenant in charge asked them to get their report filed and wait for the artist to arrive. It was past the end of the shift, but the overtime was approved. Twenty minutes later, they were seated in a quiet conference room. She asked to sit further away. Dani didn't want the artist to hear the phantom whispering to her, even though, at this point, she was reasonably confident Noah's words were only audible to her. The artist knew the exact questions to ask to help draw the facial features, even down to the bushy eyebrows. Dani and Noah watched in awe at how fast the artist recreated the suspect with plain white paper and a graphite pencil. The result is called a composite sketch.

"How do you remember so many fine details? Wasn't

it getting dark? The lighting must have been bad." asked the artist.

"Well, the gas station near the mini-mart is well-lit, and he was near there when he pulled off his mask." Dani didn't want to raise any suspicion of her ghostly whisperer.

"How does this look?" The artist turned the canvas around to reveal a perfect likeness of the robber. Dani looked at it, smiling widely, but then raised her head, distracted by some movement outside the glass conference room behind the sketch artist. It was nearly midnight, and the janitorial service had arrived. The man pushing the garbage cart around looked up into the conference room, and his face was identical to the sketch.

THREE

NO WAY BACK

T hings got extremely blurry for Dani until she was staring clearly at the *Avengers: Endgame* giant poster that was on the wall across from Noah's bed.

"What just happened?" questioned Noah.

"Our shift was over and at the worst possible time! All I needed was 30 more seconds." Dani shifted to get more comfortable in Noah's bed. "Ouch! I just put weight on my finger and totally forgot about it getting pricked."

"Why did you need 30 more seconds? The sketch artist was done."

"Remember I said I recognized the suspect?"

"Yeah."

Dani grabbed Noah's bare arm, "It's the janitor!"

"What? Are you sure?

"100%," she shook her head and looked down, "but of course, we came back before I could tell anyone."

"Not an issue; we will just reread the book." Noah jumped off the bed and grabbed the book, opening it to the chapter they were experiencing. "Here … read it."

Dani smiled excitedly, "That works?"

"We won't know until we try," responded Noah.

...I did my best to give the sketch artist everything I could remember. He was very patient with me, even though it took almost an hour.

Dani looked up sadly at Noah, "It's not working; we are still here."

"Is your bloody finger touching it?"

"Well, it's not bleeding anymore."

"Lick your finger and touch the page." Dani did as Noah instructed, but it didn't work.

"Do you have a match or a candle lighter?" She asked as she looked around the room.

"Uh, not here, maybe downstairs. Why?"

Dani searched through her school bag until her fingers bumped into something tiny and metallic. "... because I want to cauterize this safety pin in case germs are on it". Noah picked up on what she was trying to do and flew downstairs to the kitchen utility drawer.

"You kiddos want to grab some burgers downtown?" Noah's dad yelled from the family room.

"We're good. Thanks, Dad," he said as he scampered quickly up the stairs. He felt terrible being dismissive with his dad, but this was important.

"Here, found one."

Noah handed the butane gas lighter to Dani. As she started to light the pointy part of the safety pin, she had flashbacks of her firefighter adventures with the red book. She wondered if someone else borrowed the book and was now playing the role of Zach or if it was just a weird one-time fluke, given they couldn't get back into this story. Dani poked her finger wound, and a surge of heat at the wound area could be felt as the blackened needlepoint made blood visible. Noah scrunched his eyebrows and wrinkled his nose as he watched his friend make herself bleed again. She bloodied the page and began reading again. Nothing happened. They sat in defeat for about two minutes of complete silence.

"Wait, I have an idea," Noah exclaimed. "Don't watch me."

He turned his back to Dani and started doing something with his hand to his face. It seemed to take about 20 seconds. He flipped back face to face with Dani, his pointer finger sticking straight up. A golden-brown slimy booger with a streak of dark red was at the tip of his finger.

"Ewww! That's disgusting!" screamed Dani. "This is a borrowed book, and you're gonna put your bloody, gooey, revolting booger in it?"

"To be fair, you just put your blood in it, and we have already tried saliva and blood; perhaps my super smeller will give us the DNA we need. Would you rather I peed on the book?"

"OMG, Noah, if you even hint at doing that in front of me again, we are no longer friends."

Noah smirked, "I see ... but it's okay if you do it as a grown woman in front of me?" Dani didn't like that he got her there.

"Just hurry up and put that disgusting thing in the book."

Unfortunately, it didn't work, and Noah cleaned it off with a tissue at Dani's insistence.

The bike ride to Barton's Books was pleasant for a December afternoon. One advantage of living on the West Coast was mild winters. There were the occasional days of cold rain or chilly mornings, but typically, by early afternoon, the sun was shining without a cloud in the sky. This made it feel warmer than it was, and the cooler temperatures were perfect for a 30-minute bike trip.

After attempting to re-enter the story, they read through the rest of the chapter in *The Potent Police* book. Because the phantom was not in the book story, her description to the sketch artist was not as detailed, and Officer Emmy still could not recognize the suspect she thought she knew. It didn't help that she didn't turn her bodycam on, which might have helped. Bodycam is short for a wearable camera that is usually worn on the torso of the body pinned to their uniform. Officer Emmy didn't mention this to her commanding Field Training Officer (FTO). Technically, she was through her probation period after the police academy, but he was still her partner and had to report about their patrol. All this meant that Officer Hernandez never recognized the janitor, and the chapter ended with the crime unsolved. This bothered Dani and Noah, so they headed to the bookstore to see if they could get answers from the owner.

"This is exciting!" It was Dani's first visit to the bookstore. She locked her bike to Noah's in front of the entrance.

"Don't get too excited. I forgot to tell you that this woman is a bit peculiar. Be patient."

"How so?"

"You'll see; let's just take it slow. My dad told me he came here to talk to her, to get us out of our book comas. She might think we're working for the police."

"Well, technically, we are," Dani laughed. Noah smiled.

The door creaked loudly as they entered. There was no need for a door chime at this place to alert the owner about new customers. The store was dimly lit and seemingly empty. Dani picked up an earthy aroma that could only be attributed to the older book collection. As she walked down the book aisles, she could see that some books had dust that looked an inch thick, and she even saw several dusty cobwebs from abandoned spiderwebs in the shelf corners. No one greeted them, and they thought the owner was at lunch.

"I see your father was successful," a weathered voice could be heard from the back of the store.

"Hello, miss," greeted Noah.

"It's Mrs., Child; I was married once." The silhouette of a short, elderly figure appeared from the dark back corner of the store.

"Sorry, I was hoping you could ..." Noah stopped speaking as if he was frozen.

"Noah, Noah ..." Dani murmured, trying to break the moment's awkwardness.

As the light illuminated the woman, Dani noticed three medium-sized warts in various places between her forehead and cheek. Another one was on her neck. They were ghastly but not as horrifying as the final one on her nose, with hairs sticking out of it.

"Apologies again; good to see you; this is my friend, Dani. Sorry to admit, but I don't know your name."

The woman got uncomfortably close to Dani and studied her face as if she was trying to find something on it.

"You can call me Mrs. Heks. So, this is the friend who passed into the realm but has yet to be a specter."

Dani was doing her best not to retreat from the woman. The nose wart was only two inches away, and her breath smelled like rotten eggs.

"I am not completely following, Mrs. Heks, but we have a problem we need your help with," pleaded Noah.

She turned away from Dani to look at Noah. Dani's body instantly relaxed from the awkward tension.

"Yes, Child, come a little closer; my hearing is not the best." Noah begrudgingly moved within a foot of her.

"We entered the book and left too early. A crime was committed, and we know who it did, but we can't get back to tell anyone."

"Which book? Oh, the one you stole from me?" Mrs. Heks' eyes pierced at Noah's, and her nostrils flared.

"It was in your book return, and you said before you don't track—"

"That's alright, Child; we all can be a little naughty

29

sometimes," Mrs. Heks walked away from them both slowly towards the back office of the bookstore. Noah looked at Dani with a confused and agitated look.

"Just be patient. She is old and frail," Dani whispered. Noah rolled his eyes.

Mrs. Heks returned from the office, holding a small wooden box in her wrinkled hands. The box looked like it was made of dark walnut wood, almost black. There were engravings all over the box, none of which seemed to amount to anything that could be read, yet it appeared to have a strange continuous pattern.

"Please," she motioned to Dani with her hand, "come here, Child. Can I see your right hand?" Noah wondered why she would ask Dani to come to her when he was the one asking for help.

"Let me see your injured finger." She politely asked. Dani glanced at Noah and held out her finger with the cut. *How did she know?* Dani thought.

The woman pulled out two vials, one with a murky purple fluid and another with silver dust-like particles.

"Don't worry, Child, this won't hurt, but it will help your friend."

Dani was a little confused by the statement but succumbed to the woman's request. Mrs. Heks sprinkled some silver dust over the finger wound and then poured several drops of the purple liquid on top of it. The wound started to glow a deep purple-blue hue. Dani felt a sensation in her finger like when a body part falls asleep, like if you leave it in one position for too long. The cut quickly returned to its standard pink-reddish color.

"That was amazing," exclaimed Noah.

"Your phantom trip can now be resumed, but please know there could be consequences that I cannot foresee. The enchantment shall hold for but a single hour as time dances to its fleeting tune."

"How did you do that?" asked Dani.

The woman's face turned angry, and her warts appeared to almost glow red.

"What did I just say? You don't have time for stupid questions. Leave here; I have things to do."

She motioned them to the front door, moving four times faster than her usual pace. They heard the door lock behind them.

Noah and Dani rode as fast as they could back to his house. They felt like idiots for not taking the book with them. Now, they only had an hour to get back into it. The ride home was at least a half hour. Noah's face soured as they approached the railroad crossing to his house. A super long freight train was passing by and going very slow because of its heavy cargo. Unfortunately, there was no other way home, so they stopped before the crossing gate. Noah let out a long sigh, and his face appeared redder than usual. It was enhanced by the blinking red lights at the crossing.

"Noah, you need to be able to accept things you cannot change. It's unhealthy to stress about things you have no control over."

"I know, but it's easier said than done. I wish I had your self-control."

"It took everything for me not to leave the store when that weird woman wanted to look at my finger. You know she's a witch, right?"

"Um, witches don't exist, Dani!"

"Because everyone has a box with magic potions in it? Not to mention, her name means *witch*."

"Huh? Okay, I'll give you that the potion was strange, but the name?"

"*Heks* means witch in Dutch. My mom and I traveled to the Netherlands a few summers ago. I picked up some words, especially after visiting one of their haunted houses."

"Yikes, haunted houses? Remind me not to go on vacation with you!"

The train cleared, and Noah's face relaxed. His place was only 10 more minutes away, and they had another 30 minutes left on the potion timer.

They reached the front door, and Noah touched the biometric reader, but nothing happened.

"What the heck?" He blurted. He tried it three more times. "Oh, come on!" *Why does technology fail you at the worst times?* He thought.

He hoped his dad was home and knocked heavily on the door. A few seconds later, the door opened, but it wasn't his dad; it was his grandma with a big smile.

"Hello, Pumpkin," his grandma gushed with open arms.

Noah appeared happy to see her, but his body moved with impatience. This was another distraction from their mission. He smiled and politely introduced his grandma to Dani.

"Noah has your eyes," Dani stated as she reached to shake Noah's grandma's hand.

Dani felt the thin skin move over the bony structure and was careful to keep a looser grip. They didn't have time for small talk, so they quickly went inside.

"Hello, Son, isn't this a nice surprise?" asked Noah's dad. "We're going to dinner soon, so can you get ready? We can drive Danielle back to her mom's on the way to the restaurant."

Noah's body stiffened as he whispered, "We are so screwed!" But Dani saved them.

"Sir, do you mind if we finish one piece of homework

for Monday? We just got back from the library, and the research is fresh in our minds. We just need a half hour."

"I'm so glad you're teaching my son responsibility. I'll move our reservation back an hour."

Noah rolled his eyes. Dani knew Noah wasn't happy that she got credit for lying through her teeth. Regardless, she bought them time, and that was all that mattered. They had 10 minutes left before the spell wore off.

CHAPTER
FOUR

THE CLEANER

Wait a second," Noah inquired as Dani opened the blue book. "What if we get stuck in the story? My dad will probably kill me if he finds out I have another spellbound book."

"You worry too much," replied Dani. "We'll just go back to the part in the story where we started working with the sketch artist. Our shift is technically over, which is when we usually return. Besides, isn't it worth capturing the bad guy if something goes wrong?"

Noah stuttered, "Okay, but nice knowing you if we don't come back. I will be grounded for a year!"

Dani opened the book to the specific page where they met the sketch artist and started to read the paragraph. She put her spell-casted finger on the page.

"Repee Expee Ditous!" was whispered into their ears as they felt the room go nearly dark. They were back in the police station as the artist guided them to the conference room for privacy. *Yes!* Thought Dani.

"Sorry to make you wait, but do you mind if I go to the locker room to change? I've worn this uniform for nearly 12 hours now and want to get comfortable." Dani asked the artist, allowing her time to find the janitor.

"Not a problem; I'll grab a coffee and pastry from the vending machine," said the artist.

"Be careful; some of the stuff has been in that machine for months."

"What doesn't kill us makes us stronger, right?" as the artist reached into his pocket for some money.

After quickly changing, Dani and her phantom follower headed to the station's first floor, where a maintenance closet held all the cleaning supplies. Only a few officers were on the floor because this was considered the graveyard shift. Typically, a graveyard shift officer would work from 11 p.m. to 7 a.m. the next day. One of the techniques you learn at the academy is to always call for backup when you're going into a dangerous situation. This particular situation was strange, though. Dani wasn't 100% sure if the janitor she saw was the suspect from the mini-mart robbery. She wanted a better look at him before alerting her fellow officers. In some ways, she felt like Noah, the Phantom, was her backup.

"No one's here yet," said Noah. "We came down too soon. By the way, what if he recognizes you before you recognize him? That might not turn out so well."

"Well, if he were here, it would be pretty obvious right away, and I prefer to get a look at him before he's in the same room with me. I have an idea."

"Oh no...."

"Don't worry; this is sound. Remember how you have a photographic memory now?"

"Yeah ..."

"I will sit at the desk with my back to the door. You keep your silver eyes on the door. No one but me can see your phantom form. If he matches your memory, *boom!* Let me know."

"Okay, the cleaning van is pulling up; I see it; hurry, sit down!"

Just then, the front desk officer strolled to Dani's desk.

"Why are you still here?" he stated with a confused look.

Crap! Dani realized she had changed into civilian clothes for the interview, so her story to the artist checked out, but being a police officer for less than a day, she completely forgot to take her gun with her.

"Dani, the guys are getting out of the van!" Noah said with a worried tone.

"Umm, Hi! I'm just finishing up some late-night paperwork."

"Oh yeah, the boring stuff! I almost didn't recognize you without your uniform; we don't get too many pretty ladies here this time of the night. Why are you here so late? Didn't your shift end over an hour ago?"

Eww!! I am not a grown woman, Creep! Dani thought. The conversation distracted Noah from noticing the cleaning crew walking through the door.

"Evening, Officer Triton!" came from one of the two men who had just entered the station.

Noah and Dani instinctively looked at the men walking toward them from only about 30 feet away. Dani and the janitor locked eyes. His face went from pleasant to hostile. Dropping his mop, he reached behind him faster than anybody could have predicted and drew his revolver on the officers. It was seconds before the two officers realized what was happening, but not Noah. Something inside him made him move his presence in front of Dani. As the bullet fired loudly, his internal energy intensified. His invisible phantom appearance turned into a nearly sold silver form with purple accents, easily repelling the shot from striking Dani. As quickly as he changed to a solid state, he switched back to an apparition, but his head swiveled after hearing the sound of a second weapon firing. The suspect fell after being hit in the leg while his cleaning partner ran for the front door. Officer Triton quickly jumped onto the suspect and hand-cuffed him after pushing the suspect's gun away.

"Are you okay?" asked Officer Triton, looking toward Dani as he subdued the suspect and called for backup.

"Get it away, save me, please!" screamed the janitor. He didn't even fight back the officer holding him down.

"Yes, I think so," responded Dani. *What just happened? Did he see you?* Dani thought.

Noah was speechless, still trying to process the event in his head.

How did you do that? Dani continued to speak her mind to Noah.

"I don't know," he whispered back. "But it was the greatest feeling I have ever had."

Every police officer in the station rushed downstairs after hearing the shots. As they took the janitor away, he kept looking back toward Officer Hernandez. His eyes were wide open and watery. His body was visibly shivering and stumbling. Dani quickly informed the other officers that the janitor was the same person who held up the mini-mart earlier that day. As the words left her lips, Dani left the policewoman's body.

"Kids, time to go!" could be heard from downstairs as Dani and Noah sat on his bed in disbelief. Grandma and Noah's dad had been waiting patiently downstairs while the kids were supposedly finishing their homework project.

"We have to talk about his later," urged Dani.

"Sure, how about I video call you after dinner? I'm so glad you're safe. I was so scared for you. What happens if Emmy dies when you possess her?"

"I'm safe, thanks to you, Superphantom," They both smiled and headed downstairs.

Noah convinced his dad and grandma to bring Dani along. Since it was the weekend, her mom had no chores for her. Noah reminded everyone of Dani's mom's motto, *WAWPAW*, which meant *Work All Week, Play All Weekend*.

On the way to downtown Primrose Beach, Dani and Noah started whispering and giggling at each other in the back seat.

"Children, it's tough to hear when you get to my age. Do you mind speaking up?" Noah's grandma asked in a weathered voice from the front passenger seat.

"Sorry, Grandma," replied Noah, "I was talking to Dani."

"What's the big secret?" his grandma insisted.

"Oh, just school gossip, boys being boys, girls being girls, ma'am," answered Dani.

"That's sweet; you know when I was your age ... there was a young man named ..."

Dani and Noah stayed quiet to listen respectfully, but their minds were elsewhere. They could only think about what miraculously happened at the house less than 15 minutes ago. After about five more minutes, Noah's grandma's story was over, and they arrived at Belly Busters, one of their favorite local restaurants. Noah asked his dad if he could order some chicken pot pies because they wanted to hurry to the back of the restaurant to play on this old Star Wars pinball machine in the corner.

"I didn't know you liked pinball," inquired Dani.

"It's okay; I just wanted some time with you without Pops and Granny snooping."

"Noah, your grandma is old; you should appreciate the time you have with her. She won't be around forever. All of my grandparents died young, except my grandpa, but he lives in Alaska, so I never see him."

"You're right ... now, what did it feel like to hold a gun? I have never held one in real life." Noah's eyes lit up.

"Well, everything happened so fast, it's hard to remember, but it was much heavier than I expected. I feel so stupid for leaving it in the locker while we were looking for the janitor. Never mind me, thanks for saving my, I mean, Emmy's life!"

Noah pulled his shoulders back and stuck out his chest

as he responded, "No problem, it was strangely easy. I'm not even sure how I changed shape, but my phantom body felt the same way you feel when something bad is about to happen. The last time I felt that was when that bully, Kang, was about to hang me on a tree."

"This silver and purple image appeared right in front of my face; it appeared like it had fibers of metal interwoven. As quickly as it appeared, it went back to your ghost-like appearance."

"Did you see the look on the janitor's face?" recounted Noah.

"Yeah, that was scarier for me than him pulling a gun on Emmy. That guy had a tanned face that turned super white, and I even saw tears coming down his face. You are a bad-ass phantom, Noah!"

"Do you think I can do it again without someone shooting at me?"

"I don't know, but if you plan to hang around criminals, can you remind me to wear my bulletproof vest and bring my gun this time?" quipped Dani.

Noah chuckled, "Of course!"

Dani saw Noah's dad waving to him that the food had arrived at their table. As much as she wanted to keep talking, her stomach started growling, smelling all the delicious scents coming from the kitchen. As they approached the circular booth, Noah jumped inside of it quickly.

"Ahem ...," directed his grandma, "Ladies first, Noah."

"Sorry," Noah responded as he looked at his dad's reaction.

"Thank you, ma'am," Dani interrupted, "Don't worry, Noah has been quite the gentleman today in more ways than one. He is always looking out for me." Dani winked at Noah.

FIVE

WINTER BREAK

I t was the last full week of school before winter break. Noah and Dani would have two weeks off, which, of course, included Christmas and New Year. Both were looking forward to the time off but not the school exams that came before, especially Life Sciences for Noah. While at lunch, they decided to focus on studying together instead of reading the blue book, but it was super tempting not to. Noah couldn't stop thinking of what other powers awaited him as the phantom hero. He was very tempted to visit the bookstore, but the owner always creeped him out. As crazy as it sounded, he wondered if she had some phantom instruction manual.

"What do you think about taking our bikes downtown after school?" Noah asked Dani as he grabbed two more barbecue-flavored potato chips from his lunch.

"Didn't we just discuss, like literally 10 seconds ago, focusing on our exams this week?"

"What? We can't study downtown at the park near the beach? The salty air helps clear my mind."

Dani frowned, "Cut the crap, Noah, I know you want to go to the bookstore."

"Well, only if we have time after studying. You're the brainiac, so if you're not satisfied with my extensive knowledge of evolution and natural selection, we can skip the store, deal?"

"Fine, but I want to stop at Belly Busters too for a few minutes. I didn't even get a chance to play the pinball machine with all of your talking the other night."

After taking the bus home from school, they grabbed their bikes and headed downtown. Even in late December, while the air was crisp and cool, a light jacket was all that was needed. They settled on a wooden bench in the beach park with a great ocean view. The bluff was about 25 feet above the waves.

"When was the last time you talked to your mom?" inquired Dani.

"Couple nights ago, why?"

"Does she still want you to move to Arizona to live with her?"

"I don't know, she is buying a new, bigger house and asked me what color I want my room painted. I just don't see the point of reserving a room for me when I might visit ..." Noah froze, and he could feel bumps rise on the sun-drenched skin of his arms. Dani's eyes opened wide.

"Are you having a stroke, Noah? You're a bit young for that."

"Don't turn around. I think we're being watched."

"Huh ... where?" Dani started to turn her head.

"What did I just say? Sheesh! I think I see Mrs. Heks behind a tree at the corner of the park."

"You're obsessed with this woman. Are you sure? She doesn't seem like the type to go sunbathing."

"Okay ... here's what we're gonna to do. Take our trash and head toward the garbage can behind your left shoulder. It's pretty close to the tree that she's hiding behind."

Dani immediately got up and quickly scooped up the snack bags and bottles. "Be ready to call 911; she might kidnap me," she said sarcastically.

Dani moved nonchalantly toward the trash receptacles. Noah pretended to study and then glanced over the

47

cliff on the left at the crashing waves below. Despite having his head turned, he strained his eyeballs to look right and keep Dani in focus. A hunched figure emerged from the tree 15 feet away as she tossed the items in the proper bins.

"Mrs. Heks, what a surprise seeing you here," said Dani.

"I thought that was the two of you, but I wasn't sure; my eyesight is not the best these days."

"Do you come to the beach often?"

"Only the park, really; I don't want to break a hip trying to get down that cliff to the sand. I pick up spices and flavors for my stews while I am here." As she finished her sentence, Dani saw a brown beetle crawl out of her handbag.

"Noah is right over there." Dani pointed in Noah's direction, and he instantly tried to drop his shameful spy tactics. "He wanted to visit the bookstore later. Will you be there?"

"Afraid not, Child, I have some cooking to do at home of an unexpected guest. Did the finger treatment work?"

"You mean 'for an unexpected guest,'" laughed Dani.

Mrs. Heks looked confused, then smiled, "Oh, yes, Child!"

Dani motioned Noah to come over, "Yes, the treatment worked well. That's why Noah wanted to see you."

Noah waved at the store owner as if it was the first

time he saw her that day. He went to grab the book out of his backpack but hesitated. He didn't have gloves on and quickly wondered if touching the book that punctured his friend's finger was a good idea. Even if the book did prick him, he wasn't reading it, so he was safe, right? He realized he was taking too long and just grabbed his whole backpack as he approached them.

His mouth felt dry as he spoke, "Afternoon, ma'am, how are you?" He never seemed comfortable around her, no matter how often they interacted.

"Your dear friend here said you had some questions. Perhaps it's about the book in your bag there?"

"How did you know we have it?" asked Noah.

"My books are like my children. I always feel connected to them." Noah stared down as he tried to process that response.

"Can you tell me anything about controlling the supernatural being in our book trips?" Noah felt weird asking such an odd question.

"The specter relies on its host for its mastery just as the ocean's waves rely on the wind." The woman turned and scurried away before Noah could even respond.

Noah turned to Dani and raised his shoulders, "I feel that went about as well as my tricky algebra test today."

"Don't sweat it, dude; we'll figure it out. Let's finish studying; I have a date with a pinball."

They studied for their exam for another hour before

calling it quits and headed to Belly Busters. Dani showed off her mad skills on the pinball machine that Noah didn't even know she had. The more games she beat him at, the harder he tried to manipulate the device. His index fingers started to cramp up from pushing the flipper buttons harder than was needed. He tried to jiggle the machine with his body like Dani did to make the ball move in his favor, but he only ended up getting a *Tilt!* buzzer.

"Had enough?" Dani smirked.

"Where did you learn to play so well?"

"Remember how I told you that I was stuck in hotels while my mom worked as a travel nurse?"

"Yeah ... so."

"A few of the places were more like vacation resorts, and they had an arcade. I bribed my mom into giving me game money before she went to work. I think it made her feel better that she knew where I was after remote classes were finished."

"Smart!" Noah tapped his temple and pointed back to Dani.

"What's my prize for winning?"

"What are you talking about? We didn't make any bets."

"When my dad plays golf with his buddies, loser buys the others a drink, but I will settle for an ice cream cone," Dani said, grinning.

"Alright, alright, go sit down. I'll get something quickly at the counter; we have to head back soon."

Noah didn't want the waiter to come to the table because he needed a moment to check his pockets. It would've been embarrassing to order and then not have the money to pay in front of Dani. He had a sneaky suspicion he was low on funds after using most of his allowance on game tokens. He reached deep into his jeans pocket at the ordering counter and pulled the money out.

"... four, five, six dollars, and 35 cents, ugh!"

He looked at the menu board; a single cone was $4.99. He ordered one and brought it back to the table.

"Here you go, congrats on slaughtering me today."

"You didn't want one, too?" She asked.

"No, I'm good for now."

"How about we share this one? Their scoops are huge anyways."

Noah was delighted because it looked so creamy and delicious.

Dani's mom was making barbecue ribs and mashed potatoes for dinner. She asked Dani if Noah wanted to stay for dinner. Noah checked in with his dad, who was working late that night. A home-cooked meal sounded better than anything Noah could scrap together at his dad's place.

"Can I help with anything?" asked Noah as he was eager to eat.

"Sure," replied Dani's mom, "Can you set the table? The dishes are in that cabinet over there, and the silverware is in the drawer below."

Noah wished his dad was there to see how helpful he was being. He briefly thought how weird it was that you seem to become a better version of yourself when you're not at home. Perhaps home is so comforting, even your manners are laxed.

The three of them sat down at the table. Noah resisted grabbing the food first, even though the sweet, smokey smell coming off the ribs was hitting his olfactory senses so hard that his mouth started to water. He wanted to grab six ribs and an extra helping of potatoes but decided to make his plate look like Dani's.

Being a considerate person who doesn't eat like a pig is hard work!

"How are these falling off the bones so easily?" asked Noah. "I have to work pretty hard getting the meat off when my dad makes them."

"Mom, should we tell him the secret?" teased Dani.

Dani's mom laughed, "Well, your dad is going to have to make a slight investment to make his ribs better. It's called a pressure cooker. Lots of people use slow cookers to make their ribs, but that takes hours. With a pressure cooker, you can accomplish the same thing in less than an hour."

"Dang, I need to get him one for his birthday next year."

"Nice, Noah, get your dad a gift for your enjoyment; how very thoughtful of you," rebuked Dani.

"Hey, my dad likes ribs too ... can't we both enjoy the gift?"

"Alright, kiddos, I have something else that I need to talk to you about, and it's more exciting than kitchenware." Dani and Noah's eyes widened. "Winter break, as you know, starts next week. I've been asked to travel to Cancun for the week after Christmas to help with one of the hospital's ICUs."

"ICU?" inquired Noah.

"Intensive Care Unit ... it's where patients go who need critical care. I thought that since you're off school as well, Noah, you might want to join Dani and me on this trip."

"Are you being serious? Please tell me you are not joking," Noah was trying to contain his excitement. It seemed too good to be true.

Dani's mom smiled emphatically, "I promise it's real, but, of course, you will have to ask your dad first. And do you have a passport?"

"Yessss, I do, this is awesome! Wait ... how much is this going to cost?"

"My company covers the hotel, an all-inclusive resort, which means food is already included. I already bought three plane tickets because I thought Dani's brother would want to go. He is apparently too old to spend time with his boring mom and wants to hang with his friends over break, go figure. Think of it as our Christmas gift to you. You just need to bring spending money for yourself."

Before Dani could even say a word, Noah jumped from the table to call his dad.

"Hey, Son, you must really miss me ... a second call in less than an hour."

"... uh ... yeah ... I do," Noah realized that agreeing with his dad would potentially make him more accepting of the huge approval he needed. "We don't have any plans after Christmas, do we?"

"Not that I can think of, why?"

"I have the most awesome news; you are not going to believe it."

"Noah, still working here, can you get to the point?"

"I promise to follow any of your rules, and it's not going to cost you anything—"

"Noah!!"

"Dani's mom has an extra ticket to Cancun for one of her work trips, and it's the week after Christmas. Can I go? Please?"

"Do you even know where Cancun is?"

"Mexico? All I know is it's a cool, fun place, and all the food is covered, too."

"Okay, great, Son, but can we talk about it more when I get home? I need to get back to my work."

"No problem, Daddio, one more thing."

"What's that?"

"I'll also need a month's advance on my allowance," Noah's jaw tightened, and his teeth clenched together simultaneously, nervous about his father's response.

Noah's dad sighed, "Yes, let's talk later, Noah."

Noah strutted confidently back to the dinner table. Dani and her mom stared at him while awaiting his response.

Noah thrust his fists triumphantly in the air, "We're going to Mexico!"

THE PEARL OF THE CARIBBEAN

As Dani approached the Customs screening at the Cancun airport, she began to worry about the mystical book in her travel backpack. *What if the book set off their alarms?* Nothing happened going through security in the States, but maybe Customs had more sensitive machines. She glanced over at Noah, who didn't seem to have a care in the world as his head was buried in the game on his phone. *Get a hold of yourself, Dani; the real world doesn't know how to check for magic! Usually, Noah was the one who worried about stuff. Why am I?* As they passed Customs, Dani felt like a hundred eyes were staring at her. Vendors were lined up trying to get them to sign up for excursions. Her mom was an expert traveler and motioned to the kids to keep walking. There was a transportation van waiting for them outside. The driver was holding a sign with Dani's last name so they could find him in the crowd. Noah commented how he felt like a celebrity.

The site of the stone-white resort they were staying at just off the horizon was welcoming. The flight to Cancun from southern CA is less than five hours, but by the time you factor in getting to the airport early and the delays for so-called mechanical issues, it was turning out to be a long travel day. Noah's eyes were glued to the van window, which made Dani happy to be able to give him this experience.

"What do you kids want to do first?" asked Dani's mom.

"I'm up for anything that includes food," responded Noah.

"Sunset is coming soon, so we only have a little more time to get in some rays. How 'bout we hit the pool and order food there?"

Everyone agreed as the van pulled up to the circular limestone entrance of the resort. Dani took in the tropical decor as a man dressed in a linen-white shirt and grey cargo shorts opened the sliding van door for them. Mini-palm trees were lining the side of the driveway, complimented by slow-turning, low-hanging ceiling fans. The fan blades looked like wooden-carved palm leaves. An ocean breeze swept through her hair as she looked past the vast, doorless entrance to the lobby outlined with magenta bougainvillea flowers. The cool sensation only complimented the stunning visual of the turquoise-blue ocean in the far background. *What a fantastic design to see right through the hotel to the Caribbean Sea.*

"This is sick!" Noah said as he ran toward the lobby like he was trying to jump into the ocean that was hundreds of yards away.

Dani and her mom glance at each other, smiling and laughing. After a quick check-in, they changed into their swimsuits in their rooms and headed to the pool, which was placed perfectly in front of the beach. Its raised elevation gave them a nice view of the beach and the crashing waves on the rocks. There was a stairway down from the pool area right to the beach, but Dani didn't care. She wasn't a big fan of sand anyway. *It gets everywhere,* she thought. Watching the symphony of white sea foam as it drizzled off the jagged rocks from incoming waves was the therapy Dani needed after a long semester at school.

"So, I can order anything on this menu, and it's free?" asked Noah.

"Yep, but no alcoholic drinks."

"Can we get a virgin one with no alcohol? Like the one Dani showed me from her pictures of Cabo."

"Of course!" replied her mom.

They ate until their bellies hurt, lounged around, swam in the pool with a refreshing water temperature that offset the evening humidity, and drank a bunch of virgin pina coladas. Dani's mom reviewed the rules for the rest of the trip, as she would start working early in the morning. Dani watched Noah as he listened to every word, figuring he wanted to be on his best behavior for this incredible opportunity. As Dani started to fall asleep to the rhythmic ocean waves and subtle Caribbean music, she heard Noah whisper.

"This is the life!"

Sleeping in 'til 10:30 was a real treat for Dani. There was no school bus to get up early for and no chores to do either. Her mom had already left for work but left a note that ordering room service for breakfast was fine. Noah got up shortly after Dani, and they took in a gaze of the shimmering ocean water in the distance from their balcony before ordering breakfast. It was another perfect day, barely a cloud in the sky. The sun already felt hot on her face, which meant it would be a hot afternoon. Room service could be ordered right from the television in their room.

How convenient! Thought Dani.

"Wow!" said Noah, "Every time my dad and I stay in hotels, we have to call in the order over the phone. This place must cost a ton."

"Yeah, this is the first time I've seen this in all my travels; this hospital must really want my mom to help them."

"What are you getting?"

"French toast and sausage."

"Okay, can you order me the continental breakfast?"

"Consider it done. Hey, want to do a book trip after breakfast? I'm dying to learn some new phantom powers."

"How do you know the book even works here? We're so far from the bookstore and the woman's supernatural powers."

"All the better," replied Noah, "It's not her; it's the book that's magical."

Dani scoffed, "So you're the expert now?"

"Let's just give it a try. In case we get stuck, I'm writing a note for your mom with *the* word to bring us back."

"Endorshiftortus?"

"Yep, not sure how you remember that when you were in a deep coma when I said it to you. You're good, Dani."

Breakfast arrived from room service. As they opened the metal warming covers, Dani's stomach started to growl at the sight of freshly cut pineapple, cantaloupe, and bright red strawberries. She looked over to Noah's tray and then back to hers in a confused manner.

"What's wrong?" asked Noah.

"Nothing, they forgot to bring jelly for my croissant. I'll just get it from the front desk ... calling room service again will take too long. I'll be right back," as she skipped toward the hotel door.

Dani strolled through the lobby in her robe and slippers and thought she had forgotten her room key. She reached frantically into her soft, terry-clothed pocket and felt a slim card just as she reached the hotel clerk's counter.

"Are you okay, young lady?" A tall woman with a very bright shade of orange lipstick greeted her with a smile.

"Oh ... yes, crisis averted," Dani smiled back, "... but I have a small request. Room service forgot to bring jelly with my breakfast."

"I sincerely apologize. Let me grab some in the back for you, one moment."

As she disappeared through a door behind the counter, a tiny white Pomeranian appeared around the corner of the front desk.

"Well, hello there, Cutie!" Dani crouched down to pet the small, friendly pup.

A few seconds later, she heard, "Miss, here you are, and I see you met Frosty."

"Yes, is it a she?"

"You guessed right. Would you like to give her a treat? She loves blueberries. I just grabbed some from the breakfast supply." The clerk handed Dani a handful.

Frosty started wagging her tail excitedly and started reaching up to Dani, balancing on just her hind legs.

"Here you go, girl," Dani extended her cupped hand to the dog. "I didn't know the hotel allowed dogs."

"Technically, we don't, but I had to take her to the vet on the way to work today, so my boss said it was cool as long as she stayed behind the counter. So much for following that rule."

Frosty finished the blueberries before the clerk could even finish her sentence. She licked the extra blue juice from Dani's palm. Dani pet her one last time on the head, grabbed the jelly on the counter, and turned back toward the elevators.

"Thank you, ma'am, and nice meeting you, Frosty."

By the time Dani returned, Noah had scarfed down his entire breakfast and was waiting on the bed with the blue book beside him.

"Thanks for waiting for me. I guess I don't get to try the French toast," Dani held up the empty white plate with only a layer of syrup remaining.

"Sorry, I was hungry, and you were taking forever."

"I was gone exactly 8 minutes, Noah!"

"So ... you are going to read again, right? I want to be the phantom again."

"Not sure it matters, honestly; I think we're tied to the characters we came in as initially." Dani licked the jelly off her fingers and happily ate her croissant.

"Maybe, but I have more experience in this, so can we just follow my lead?"

"Okay, but I don't want to poke my finger again and bleed. I'm just going to try with the saliva already on my fingers.

Dani jumped on the bed and quickly glanced over to the nightstand to ensure the instructions were clear for her mom. If they got stuck, she wanted her mom to be able to break the spell. She began to read from the police book, but this time, something different happened.

"Poofwoof!"

Dani heard a different word whispered, and her skin immediately had the feeling you get when all of your body hair stands on its end from a chilly spike of air conditioning. Even the hair on her head felt like it moved. Her vision seemed a little blurrier than usual, and objects were strangely colored violet-blue, yellow, and gray.

"Oh no!" gasped Noah.

Dani turned toward Noah and could see his phantom form, so she knew she was back in the book, but why was she observing him from two feet off the ground?

"You okay, Boy? You looked spooked," came from a woman in uniform sitting at a desk. She patted Dani on her head.

"You're a dog," whispered Noah.

SEVEN

KIP THE K-9

What? How did this happen? Of course ...
Why did I let that dog eat out of my hand?

Dani could feel her tail wagging, but it felt totally involuntary. She also had this strong attachment to the woman sitting beside her, which made her feel very safe. Her sense of smell was in overdrive. She recognized the smell of coffee from a desk at the back of the room. This was mixed with the faint scent of fresh gunpowder that appeared to be in an adjacent room. Dani's trip last year with her dad to watch him shoot guns at her uncle's range in Montana was the only way she knew that smell.

"Your harness says you're part of the K-9 unit. So, how does it feel to be a police dog?" Noah asked.

It's a good thing you can hear my thoughts because I doubt phantoms speak dog.

"You never know. I dare you to ask the officer next to you to take you for a walk."

... and if I am a talking dog, what do you think the next step is for them? Probably the dog funny farm.

"Come on, Dani, live a little, I'll protect you," Noah assured her.

Will you please figure out what our mission is so we can get out of here? I am smelling something weird on my paw and feel like I should lick it. I'm afraid to think what my paw last touched.

Noah scanned around the officer's metal desk to gather clues, like maybe a schedule for the day. As he did, a man walked right through him.

"Woah, is your desk under a vent? It's freezing right here," the man remarked to the officer sitting next to Dani.

"Not that I know of; I'm perfectly comfortable. It must be your old age, Cap," she rebutted.

He moved around her chair and started petting Dani on her back. "... and how are you, Kip? Ready to fight crime again this afternoon? I have an assignment for you and Officer Mason."

Dani had mixed feelings about being touched. She was never a big fan of family hugs, but oddly, a stranger's pull on her dog hair was very calming.

The captain continued. "We got a tip from one of our CIs that a plane from Vancouver is landing at Sutter Airfield, the one near the mall. We need a team to intercept so Kip can tell us if they are bringing drugs into the country."

"Why are we handling that? Isn't that the DEA's territory?" Office Mason inquired.

"They won't make it here in time; the flight is due to arrive in less than an hour."

"We're on it, boss. Kip, come, let's go potty."

Potty? What am I, four years old? Thought Dani as she followed the officer as she was commanded.

"Well, actually, I believe you are that old in dog years," chuckled Noah, "I have this connection to you being your personal, spiritual guard, and I can sense it. It's similar to how another dog can do it, only I don't have to sniff your butt like they do."

"Gross, Noah, don't you come near my butt!"

Noah let out a hearty laugh. It seemed so loud that Dani swiveled her head around to check that no one heard.

"What's so funny?" She asked.

"You are!" Noah exclaimed. "I heard your thought right before you spoke it, and guess what? Your words weren't English. Great bark, by the way. It is very alpha-dog like."

The officer led them to the side yard of the police station that had a dog run.

"Kip, go potty." Office Mason instructed.

This is so embarrassing; Dani drooped her snout as she approached the grass.

On the way to the airport, Dani wondered how much they would need to use her. Would she just sniff some suitcases and let the humans do the rest, or would she have to pursue the suspects?

She had a prior memory from her host that involved a chase over a snow-laden field on a chilly Chicago winter evening. Kip was in pursuit of an armed man and appre-hended him by locking his jaw around the criminal's wrist. This was the best place to bite because the rest of his body was covered with thick winter clothing. This caused him to drop his gun and give the handler enough time to catch up and cuff the perpetrator. Besides the great satisfaction, Kip had yummy memories of devouring a large, juicy piece of meat that included a crunchy bone that evening. It was an interesting perspective for Dani to realize that even dogs have long-term memories of positive events like helping their owners or getting a special treat.

"Did you understand all that police talk earlier?" Noah asked as he tried to get comfortable in the small, gray, powder-coated transport space in the back of the police SUV.

The vehicle's backseat space was modified with a metal cage-type structure with a rubber floor for carrying dogs. Dogs need less space than humans. The phantom was the size of a large human. Dani watched in amazement as the apparition squeezed into a six-inch cage opening that led to the vacant front passenger seat. Officer Mason involuntarily shivered from the sudden frigid air next to her.

"How did you do that?" gasped Dani.

"Honestly, I don't know. I felt super cramped and focused on the big front seat."

"You know you just figured out another phantom power, right?"

Noah took a second to respond. "I thought this book trip would be a waste of time, but it seems to have served some purpose."

"About your police talk question, a CI is short for confidential informant. These informants provide information to the police in exchange for a reduced punishment for their crimes."

"—and you know this how?"

"Don't you remember when you were a firefighter? You possess the body and get all their memories too, which for me includes Officer Hernandez's academy training."

"Oh ... I thought since you have such a small dog brain, you would be dumber."

Dani snarled while growling, "You're lucky you don't have a body for me to bite!"

"Calm down back there, boy! We're almost there," interjected Officer Mason to stop all the indecipherable barking.

Sutter Airfield was a smaller airport with only a couple of plane hangars. It was mainly used for flight instruction and training. The runways were not long enough for large commercial passenger planes. Dani saw a sea of single-propeller planes parked around the runway with various markings and color striping. About half a dozen sleek planes with dual jet engines were in one section of the airfield. They looked expensive, and Dani assumed only the rich could afford to fly them. Officer Mason's SUV was accompanied by two more police cars. One of the hangar's custodians motioned the vehicles to park inside the hangar. This would keep the team out of site from the air as the plane in question was expected to arrive any minute.

Officer Mason got out and opened the door for Kip, but Dani knew not to move unless commanded. Kip went through K-9 training that taught him to only respond to commands from his handler. His handler is the officer that he's assigned to. The most important part of the training was learning that, above anything, protecting his handler was the priority. As Dani watched the rest of the officers exit their vehicles and gather together for a briefing, one of them looked very familiar.

"Noah, look at the officer on the far right; doesn't she look familiar?"

"Duh, of course, it's Officer Hernandez."

"You know my eyes aren't as good as a human, much less an enhanced silver-eyed phantom."

"Point taken. Maybe our mission is to protect her," suggested Noah.

"Good thinking, partner," Dani raised her canine ears to ensure she didn't miss any cues from her owner.

The team of officers checked their belts to make sure their guns were unsnapped from their holsters in the event they were needed. One of them pointed to the runway as Dani heard the distinct noise of jet engines winding down to indicate a plane coming to a stop on the airstrip. Officer Mason signaled to her K-9 partner to come to her side.

Dani jumped out of the vehicle before Noah even knew what was happening.

"Woah! Woah! Dani!" yelled Noah, as he was quickly sucked out of the vehicle due to his sorcerous attachment to Dani's canine body.

The officers walked toward the passengers exiting the plane. Kip followed closely behind Officer Mason. The passengers started exiting slower as they appeared surprised by the encounter.

"Anybody else inside?" asked the police sergeant.

A tan, scruffy-faced man with broad shoulders wearing a white-linen sports coat grinned, "Just the pilot ... everything alright, officers?"

"Customs called in sick. Can we see your passports and papers? Also, is your luggage up front or in the back?"

"There must be some mistake, sir. We are just here to refuel on our way to The Sunshine State. Wouldn't we go through Customs there?"

"Florida, huh, let me see your flight plan," the sergeant raised his hand, palm up, bending his fingers toward him in a continuous curling motion.

"Let me retrieve it from the pilot. He is prepping for our next flight."

The large man walked up the short stairs to the entry opening and headed left to the cockpit. This left two men outside with the four officers. Officer Hernandez had her back to the plane. Seconds later, Dani's super hearing recognized a distinctive noise she had been trained on: a rifle being cocked. Kip let out the precise series of barks to inform his handler. Officer Mason knew precisely what Kip was telling her, quickly glanced away from the Canadians, and saw a muzzle sticking out of the cockpit window directed at the back of Officer Hernandez's head.

"Everyone down now!!!" Officer Mason yelled as she crouched and ran up the stairs to the plane. "Freeze!" as she directed her aim at the two men in the front of the aircraft.

Outside, the rest of the officers subdued and began handcuffing the other two travelers. No shots were fired, preventing a catastrophe. Kip had followed his handler in case she required assistance, and once inside the plane, the sensors in his nose exploded into action. Kip started digging and pawing at the forward luggage compartment.

"Dang, Dani ... you saved the officers, found the drugs, and didn't even need my help."

Noah read Dani's thoughts as she barked. "I have so much more respect for these police dogs. We are amazing, but I still miss being a tween. Why aren't we going back?"

The DEA arrived to find over 300 boxes of Adderall used to treat ADHD. After testing, it was discovered the pills were laced with fentanyl. Dani overheard one of the agents mention that it takes only an amount of fentanyl equal to 10-15 grains of salt to kill someone. He also reported how so many middle-grade and high-school kids died from these versions of Adderall, not knowing it was laced with a lethal drug. Dani had seen other kids at school trying to help their classmates with pills to focus. She made a mental commitment to spread the word to her classmates never to accept pills from anyone except their parents. Her dog hair stood on end as she finished her thoughts.

CHAPTER EIGHT

Savage Xavage

D ani and Noah stared at each other as their vision became clearer. Dani looked anxious as she quickly slid her hands over the contours of her face and body.

"I'm me again!"

"Thank goodness. I got tired of listening to your animal thoughts," scoffed Noah.

"Mm-hmm, it scared you that they were more complex than your human boy thoughts, didn't it?"

"I must admit, your ideas to bring awareness to our

school about drug dangers are admirable. I'll help you; maybe we can make some posters for the hallways."

Dani smiled. "I'm just happy no one got hurt. Was there even a dog story in the enchanted book?"

"We should check, but I know you saved Officer Hernandez's life. She was right in the firing line. I bet she never knew how close she came to having her head explode like a pumpkin blast."

"Leave it to you, Noah, to come up with the gory visuals."

"What? You've never been to a pumpkin patch where they have corn mazes and pumpkin cannons?"

"Yeah, but I remember decorating pumpkins, not destroying them."

"Your loss. Hey, I'm hungry again; want to head down to the buffet?"

"One second," said Dani as she quickly scanned through the book, making sure not to read out loud. "Found it!"

"Found what?" exclaimed Noah.

"This chapter talks about the drug bust. Emmy was hit in the shoulder!"

"Are you kidding?"

"No, it took her three months to recover," said Dani.

Noah started to pet Dani on the head and grabbed the book. "You were a good dog, and now you deserve a treat!" He tossed the blue book in his suitcase and headed for the door.

"Aren't you forgetting something?" Dani cautioned as she grabbed the room key and her wallet while motioning to the nightstand.

Noah looked over and saw a hotel-branded notepad with the instructions for Dani's mom lying on the glass table. "Oops, yeah, this will be hard to explain." He tore off the page from the pad, re-opened the book in his suit-case, and placed the note inside the cover.

The Spanish-tiled hallway from the elevator to their hotel room was easily a couple hundred yards with one minor turn at about three-quarters of the way there.

"I'll race you to the room. Whoever loses has to buy the winner something of their choice from the gift shop," challenged Noah.

"You really want to do this after we just stuffed ourselves with burgers and fries? What's the gift limit?"

"20 bucks?"

"How are we going to know when to start? It can't be one of us that will give the starter an advantage," questioned Dani.

"Jeez, do you have to make everything so rule-orien-tated?" Noah thought for a moment, then heard a hotel door close. "That's it! The next hotel door we hear close is our starter pistol, got it?" Dani nodded.

Noah badly wanted to win, especially since he only brought a couple hundred dollars in spending money for the trip and was already down to eighty. He had decided to get a gift for his dad for letting him go on the trip and didn't realize how expensive the hotel gift shop shirts were, as were the snacks. He also wanted to show Dani he was better than her at something after the beating she gave him on the pinball machine at Belly Busters.

THUD!

Dani leaped forward and was quickly four feet in front of Noah from the start. Noah was shocked to see this, but it only heightened his enthusiasm. He started raising his knees higher with each step to gain more ground. The two were now neck and neck. A house-keeping cart surprised them as they reached the turn, and it blocked half of the hallway. Lucky for Noah, it was on Dani's side, and he took advantage by going through the opening on the right side first. Their room was getting closer; his legs burned with each step, but he kept pushing himself, not knowing how far back Dani was. He treated the room like it was first base in one of his baseball games. He was going to blow past it to keep his speed, and hopefully, that meant he was still safe, just like in the sport. As Noah passed the room, Dani slowed to tag the door.

"Woo hoo! You missed the room, Noah!" Dani gushed with her hands on her knees, trying to catch her breath.

"No, I didn't," replied Noah as he walked back toward her. "I reached the room first!"

"Sure, you did. You would've kept running if I didn't stop at the room."

"Remember the rules? I said we'd race to the room, not tag the door."

Their hotel room door suddenly opened with Dani's mom in the entryway.

"What is going on out here?" she asked.

"Nothing, ma'am, your daughter owes me twenty bucks."

Dani shook her head and rolled her eyes while trying to get a few more words out between catching her breath, "only on a technicality. Wait ... aren't you supposed to still be at work, Mom?"

"They gave me the afternoon off and thought we could do something fun together. Have you two ever heard of Xavage Park?" Both of them shook their heads. "It's an adventure park not far from us. It has zip-lining, jet boating, white-water rafting, monster trucks, and more."

"Savage! Sounds dangerous, I'm in ... Dani?"

"It's pronounced Xavage; the 'X' is pronounced like the letters 'Sh.'"

"Who cares? Let's go!" yelled Noah.

"Fantastic," said Dani's mom, "I assume you guys just

came back from lunch by the mustard on Noah's cheek; I'll pick up something to go on the way to the lobby. Please wear closed-toed shoes and lock up your luggage before we go."

Noah happily complied, not wanting the book to fall into the hotel staff's hands. He was excited about the park, which made him briefly think about his dad. Was his dad working even more hours since Noah was not there to be taken care of? He wished his dad could be there with him to go on the rides. He needs to work less and have more fun. Noah decided to call him as he stepped out on the balcony.

"This is a nice surprise!"

"Hey, Dad, how are you? Cancun is awesome; you have to come here someday."

"That's good to hear. I was there many years ago. Your mom and I went on our honeymoon. Are you following the rules and using your manners?"

"Yes, Dad, you know me?"

"Exactly, which is why I am reminding you."

Noah chuckled. "Are you working a gazillion hours this week?"

"Actually, the week after Christmas is slower. I took a few days off and golfed; the weather was quite warm for winter."

"Good for you, well ... I have to go; we're leaving for an adventure park soon. Pet Mumu for me."

"Sounds fun, and I will. Love you, Son."

"Back at you, Dad." Noah was no longer concerned about this dad as he hung up, knowing he was also taking time out to relax this week. His eyes stared momentarily at the sparkling blue pool and lush palm trees below their balcony. He loved staying in fancy resorts.

During the trip back to the resort, Dani and Noah couldn't stop talking about the park. The weather was nearly perfect, especially for going on water rides. The warm sun and higher humidity kept them from feeling cold when they got wet. Neither had ever been river rafting, and the park's course was a great introduction.

"Did you know that California has Class 5 rapids?" Noah boasted.

"What class was the one in the park?"

"I read the brochure; it was a Class 3. I heard you must take a swim test before you go on Class 5 rapids since you might fall out of the boat more easily."

"You know, kids, there are some good rivers in Northern California, like the American River; it has multiple forks," interjected Dani's mom. "We can make a trip up there someday if you want."

"That would be fun, Mom," replied Dani.

"Yeah, we can bring my dad, too; he loves doing things outdoors," said Noah.

Dani's mom only had to work one more morning at the hospital as the admissions had slowed during the week. This left her half of the week to hang out with the kids before they had to leave for home that Saturday. Noah thought what a fantastic job she had. Not only did they bring her to a warm, tropical place, but she also got a mini, free vacation. They spent the rest of the week checking out some of the shopping and eateries downtown, going to the beach, and visiting the ruins in Tulum. Noah realized that getting a Cancun shirt for his dad from one of the street vendors was exponentially cheaper than the resort gift shop. He was super happy to be able to return the gift shop shirt and save $40.

GTA

T he trip back to California felt long for Dani. She calculated the travel hours, and the time to get home wasn't much longer than it was to get to Cancun. Perhaps the excitement of going somewhere different made the time pass faster. Although she enjoyed learning at school, the thought of early mornings, home-work, and cramming for tests again in a few days was unpleasant. She looked over enviously at Noah, who was utterly absorbed in his Triassic Traveler game on his phone. *Why can't I be more like him and enjoy the moment instead of worrying about things in the future?* It was almost 11 p.m. now while they drove home from the airport.

"Mom, can Noah just sleep over? His dad is probably sleeping already," Dani inquired.

"Way ahead of you, Honey. I texted him when we landed that I would bring Noah back in the morning after breakfast. He was totally fine with that."

This got Noah's attention from his phone game, and he grinned at Dani. Dani smiled back, and they simultaneously both whispered to each other.

"Story time!"

Dani's house had a separate room for entertainment that included a sofa with a pull-out memory foam bed. Her mom set it up for them, and Noah volunteered to get hot chocolates for them in the kitchen.

"Don't stay up too late, kiddos; you've had a long travel day," Dani's mom insisted as she walked out of the room.

"We won't," replied Dani.

Dani didn't want to take any chances this time on turning into an animal. She washed her hands thoroughly in the bathroom and prepared her needle and lighter to sanitize the needle. She got cozy in the bed, propped her fluffy pillows up behind her head, and brought the down comforter close to her chest. The room had one of those fake fireplaces attached to the wall, generating different color flames. Noah seemed amazed by it and turned on its timer before hopping into the bed next to Dani. They started reading a chapter labeled "Grand Theft Auto." They heard a whisper of "Plasmador" as the magic took them back into the book.

Dani breathed a noisy sigh of relief after realizing she was sitting on a chair beside other officers and could see her human hands.

"Am I boring you, Officer Hernandez?" After the sergeant called her out, the entire roll call audience turned back to look at Dani. Officer Hernandez's face went from light brown to beet red.

"No, sir, I apologize. I was thinking of something I forgot at home this morning," replied Dani.

"Well, maybe you can think more about how we are going to solve our year-over-year triple-digit percentage growth in motor vehicle thefts," rebuked the sergeant. "The Superintendent is furious after seeing our CompStat reports, folks. He reminded us there was a big increase last year too and questioned what we're going to do about it."

The Superintendent is the highest rank in the Chicago police department. Large metropolitan cities will typically have a different level than smaller rural cities. In the smaller cities, the Police Chief is the highest.

"Nice going, Dani. We haven't even been here two minutes, and you're already in trouble," teased Noah as he took in the surroundings.

That was embarrassing, thought Dani. *Get out of my head, Noah, and pay attention so we can figure out why we are here.*

The sergeant continued, "We are officially starting a public awareness campaign, an undercover sting operation, and an auto theft task force. Since Officer Hernandez seems bored, she and her partner will join that operation."

Dani looked over at Officer Jones, who was mouthing "thank you" with an annoyed face. Dani recalled several instances from Officer Hernandez's short time with the police district where she seemed to be picked on unnecessarily. She started to feel like it was because she was a woman, one of only three in this District. Dani vowed to kick butt at this new assignment so they could do nothing but praise her.

"The additional details for your assignments are on the bulletin board. Stay vigilant, stay safe, and watch each other's backs." The sergeant ended the roll call.

Officer Jones and Dani walked over to the Sting Operation board instructions. They were briefing in 10 minutes, and it was going down that evening. Officer Jones seemed pleased that it would mean overtime, which he had been wanting so he could save extra money. Dani felt better that she caused them to be included.

The sting operation was to monitor and possibly enter a warehouse for a bust in the 8th District but near the 7th District border to which Officer Hernandez was assigned. The warehouse was suspected of pulling in newly stolen vehicles, stripping them down for parts resale, or reselling them to criminals to use as a getaway car in another crime. The Chicago Police Department was divided into 22 districts covering a 237-square-mile jurisdictional area. For these operations, Districts often collaborated, especially when the entire department was trying to make an impact on the city's crime statistics.

Their regular shift was low-key. The most exciting thing that happened was a stop at an apartment complex to take a report on a domestic disturbance. Once Dani and her partner arrived and started taking down the details, the husband and wife started crying and felt terrible for involving the authorities. They made up and invited Dani and her partner to stay for their meatloaf dinner, which was awkward. Of course, they politely declined.

After grabbing a quick bite to eat at Checkers, a fast-food joint, they joined the other units at the meeting point near the warehouse around 8 p.m. Officer Jones and

Dani's job was to stay in their vehicle about four blocks away, listen on the radio frequency to see if they were needed should the undercover officers decide to move in for arrests. Around 9:10, the police radio blipped.

"We have two vehicles spotted about to enter the garage. One appears to be a Kia, and the other a Hyundai. Bird's Eye is photographing the license plates now." The officer reported on the operation frequency.

Dani immediately knew the probability of them being stolen was higher. The briefing on the operation indicated that those two car makers made up nearly half of all motor vehicle thefts last year. She also remembered reading that Bird's Eye was the codename for the officer on the building roof across from the warehouse with a high-powered telescopic camera.

More chatter came over the radio. "Plates secure, checking with Dispatch. The garage is opening, and there appears to be a heavy amount of work being done inside and at least a dozen other vehicles."

About seven minutes later, "Code 2, Code 2, stolen plates confirmed!!"

"Here we go!" Officer Jones commented as he put the vehicle in gear.

"Dani, I think I remember how to make my body impenetrable again. I'll try and stay ahead of you," Noah proclaimed.

Okay, but don't forget, they can also see you when you transform, just use it if you sense a shoot-out.

They could see some occupants taking a smoke break outside as they approached the warehouse while the door was still open. It would be much easier if they could enter the building for the arrest before the garage closed. The men sensed street noise and didn't want to take any chances. They tossed their cigarettes on the street and hurried inside. The garage started to close. A second later, a modified police SUV darted out of an alley toward the garage. The officer was able to stop it right under the large door.

When you pass the threshold, garage doors often have sensors that detect an obstruction, which sends the door in reverse to open again. This old warehouse door did not, and instead, it came crashing down on the hood of the SUV. Dani was surprised it didn't do much damage from afar and figured the department's vehicle modifications were tank-like. Officer Jones and Dani were a few seconds behind the SUV. They were about to pull in behind when suddenly, the SUV was shot back toward the street like a cannon. The four tires made a sharp, staccato sound like a thunderclap through the air. The tires flattened as they hit the asphalt, their rubbery skin surrendering to the unyielding solidity of the pavement. The large SUV skipped backward while tilting side to side, almost rolling over. Officer Jones slammed on the brakes, nearly missing an impact with the tossed vehicle.

"What the hell was that?" yelled Noah, observing in the backseat.

"Oh my God," Officer Jones exasperated, "they're so lucky they weren't exiting the vehicle when that happened."

Dani jumped out of their patrol car. She could see the garage finish closing out of the corner of her eye. She ran to the damaged SUV.

"You guys okay?" She shouted through the closed window. The officers seemed stunned but gave a thumbs up to signal their physical state.

"Dani, get me close to the garage. I have an idea," Noah instructed.

By now, another patrol SUV had pulled up, and officers exited to start surrounding the warehouse. Preliminary scouting had shown there were only three people in the warehouse. There were six officers outside, which was enough to overtake the facility. Dani got close to the garage, and she watched as Noah made his special move to squeeze his gaseous body down into an opening in the side of the garage door that was only a few inches wide.

Now, on the inside, Noah looked around to try and figure out what happened. Two men were scrambling back and forth, trying to secure their fake license plates, put away their stripping equipment, and load hand weapons. But there was nothing big enough to catapult the officer's SUV backward. All the vehicles were smaller, two-door foreign coupes. Just then, a bearded man with a cigar in his mouth appeared from behind some pallets with crates. Behind him was a being twice his size, with an appearance as if Noah was looking into a mirror.

"Kang, secure the perimeter," the bearded man ordered.

"What? Kang? No!!"

Just as Noah spoke, the being heard and looked in his direction. He immediately shot a blast of energy from his two claws that had the brilliance of the sun but silver in color with fast-moving black particles. It hit Noah dead-on and completely eviscerated him into nothing.

CHAPTER
TEN

A SHADOW FROM YESTERDAY

D ani came to suddenly and looked over to Noah, who appeared still. She leaned over and shook Noah.

"Noah, get up, get up! We came back early. Are you okay?" Dani started to shake Noah harder, this time with both hands. Noah's eyes opened slowly.

"I had the worst dream ... wait, oh my gosh ... we were book traveling."

"Something went super wrong. There was a loud bang, and the metal door buckled outward with a five-foot dent. What happened in there?" Dani asked.

Noah was silent for a few seconds while he tried to recall the events. "We've messed up everything!"

He sat up in the bed and put his head down into his hands, shaking uncontrollably.

"Noah, calm down. What did you see?"

"Kang."

"What do you mean you saw Kang? From our school?"

"Yes."

"Are you sure? He's still missing." Dani insisted.

"No, you don't understand; he is a phantom now; don't ask me how. But he is bigger, faster, and stronger than me. He hit me with some sort of power burst that disintegrated my phantom body. It hurt like heck too. I bet you any money he's the one who hurled that SUV back."

"Oh no, the officers have no idea what they're up against if Kang can do those things to real objects."

"Yeah, and what's worse, he's taking orders from one of the perpetrators. Kang is like their bodyguard now," replied Noah.

"How did Kang become a phantom in the first place? Do you think he found Barton's Books? He doesn't appear to be the type of kid that likes to read."

"I have no idea! We have to go back to Mrs. Heks and see if she can help." He picked up the blue book and opened it to where they were reading, skimming further into the chapter. His stomach started to feel queasy. "I think I'm gonna be sick."

"Why?" Dani grabbed the book to look.

"The story ends with them arresting the carjackers. There is no way that happened now with Kang involved. We also need to check the library archives at school."

"Alright, listen," Dani tried to talk as calmly as possible. "We won't know anything till we check the archives and find a way back. Remember the magic silver dust?"

"Sure, what if Mrs. Heks doesn't have anymore?"

"—relax, Noah. Let's get some sleep and work on it tomorrow."

Dani turned on her side and pulled up the covers. Noah lay on his back, staring at the ceiling. While he knew Dani had made some good points, it was difficult not to worry. The display of power that Kang showed as a phantom was something not to be trifled with. He had to figure out how to get the same or even more potent abilities when he's in phantom form. *What would be the point of jumping back into the same story if he was inferior to Kang?* He tried to recall his thoughts when he discovered his power to become a human shield or fit into tiny openings. His mind was racing but also drifting into dreamland as it had been an extraordinarily long day.

The following day, Noah woke up to the deliciously mouthwatering smell of bacon. It awakened his taste buds and ignited the hunger in his stomach. He left the sofa bed slowly to avoid waking Dani and walked to the kitchen.

"Good morning, Noah. How'd you sleep?" Asked Dani's mom.

"Decent, thank you. Oh, I wanted to thank you for the great trip."

"It was my pleasure. Glad you had fun; what was your favorite part?"

"The adventure park was a blast, but would it be bad to say I loved the all-you-can-eat buffets too?"

Dani's mom laughed, "Of course not. That's part of the vacation benefits, and you are a growing boy." She placed a plate of the fluffiest scrambled eggs Noah had ever seen, crispy bacon, and buttered toast on the table.

"Thank you for breakfast. This looks fantastic."

"I'm sure your dad and puppy are anxious to see you. I will run you over to your house after breakfast."

Just then, Noah remembered what had happened the previous night and was concerned if their book trip had changed history. He had to learn his phantom powers quickly.

"Ma'am, do you mind if I ask you a question?"

"You just did," Dani's mom grinned.

"Right, okay, how do adults figure out what skills they have so they know what they're good at for work?"

"Well, I didn't expect such an in depth question at 9 a.m., but good thing I've already had two cups of coffee. Sometimes it's luck, but I think it's mostly trial and error. I always tell Dani to try new things because you never know when you might do something that clicks with your personality and talents."

A bit deflated, Noah's face soured, "... but that could take a long time, right?" He didn't have time to figure out if he could be a mighty phantom.

"Sure, it can, but here's another tip. Follow your heart. Even if other people, including those close to you, tell you differently, follow what makes you happy and avoid the things that make you miserable. Does that make sense?"

"Yes, it does."

Noah stared for a minute at his plate, realizing he had devoured his food. At that moment, it hit him like a punch to the gut, or maybe it was the pain in his stomach from eating too fast.

Go with my feelings!

Noah realized that most of the time when he was a phantom, he was observing what was around him but not using his feelings to control his actions. The one time he did feel something was when he protected Dani from that crazy janitor. Just because he was connected to Officer Hernandez didn't mean he had to be a follower. He could be a leader and lead with his hunches.

"Are you okay? I think I lost you for a few minutes there," Dani's mom questioned.

"I'm fine! Thanks for the great advice."

Noah grabbed his suitcase from the entertainment room. Dani was still fast asleep, so he tiptoed around, watching her intently to see if he was disturbing her. The drive to Noah's house was only about 10 minutes on the weekend. Dani's mom dropped off Noah at the end of the cul-de-sac. Noah could see Mumu jumping up and down on the couch near the front window as he approached the door. He pressed his thumb against the fingerprint reader. When the door opened, he was almost knocked over by the 75-pound gray and white beast as his front paws reached up for Noah's shoulders.

"Whoa! Now, now, Mumu. I missed you too!" Noah petted Mumu's head swiftly as if trying to get all the missed petting from the week in one loving session.

"Hey Son, good to see you! You look very tan. Did you wear sunblock?"

"Hi Dad, of course! We spent a lot of time outside."

"That's good to hear. I was hoping you didn't stay in the room the whole time playing games on your phone. What are your plans today? Tomorrow is the first day back to school after break, so I know you don't have homework."

"Nope, I'm all yours, Dad; what did you have in mind?"

"Remember that vacant store downtown?"

"The one where that woman vanished, leaving her baby like a year ago?"

"Yep, they leased it to a new tenant. They converted it into an arcade with batting cages in the back."

"What? Awesome!"

"Did you eat breakfast?"

"Yep, Dani's mom was a great host, and if you're wondering, I put my manners on overdrive," Noah clarified with a smile.

"Happy to hear, Son. While you were vacationing, I've been practicing Skee-Ball, so I think you'll be in trouble."

Noah and his dad used to play Skee-Ball competitively at a bowling alley by their old house before they moved.

"They have Skee-Ball? Want to wager on your skills?" Noah challenged.

"You spent all of your vacation money, didn't you?"

"Yeah," Noah unzipped his suitcase and found what he was looking for after a few seconds of searching through balls of clothes. "... but it was worth it!"

He tossed a cotton shirt at this dad. His dad spread out the shirt and realized it was his size. It had a scenic palm tree design with the word "Cancun" on it.

"That was very thoughtful of you; thank you, Son."

He reached over to Noah and hugged him tight.

Mumu got jealous and jumped up on them. They laughed heartily.

CHAPTER
ELEVEN

WHAT THE HEKS

The Monday back from winter break was chaotic for the kids at Dani and Noah's school. It was as if everybody had gotten amnesia over the short break. Many of them forgot their gym clothes, and some, to Dani's disdain, had failed to take their clothes out of their bags to wash during the break. They still decided to wear them to class for fear of getting in trouble. Dani endured an entire period with the stench of stale body odor, damp socks, and the faint tang of mildew. Her gym class was before lunch, and the horrid smell ruined her appetite.

This worked out for her friend, Kari, who forgot her lunch bag on her kitchen counter. Dani began to share her lunch with Kari just as Noah found them and sat down.

"What's up, ladies?" said Noah.

"Your friend, Dani, is awesome-sauce; she's saving me from starvation," replied Kari.

"Yeah, my friend, Parker, forgot his lunch too but is getting cafeteria food."

"That food is so bad for you. It's salty, and I found a hair on my pizza slice the last time I went through the line," Kari proceeded to wrinkle her nose and point her index finger into her mouth like she was pretending to make herself gag.

"Eww!!" commented Dani.

"Dani, do you want to meet in the library in a little bit to work on our project?" Noah winked but made sure Kari didn't see him do it.

"We only get a half-hour lunch break; you two should relax," responded Kari. Dani and Noah looked at each other, "We got enough of that in Cancun last week!" replied Noah.

"Wow, I was wondering why you both look so tan," said Kari.

Kari left to catch up with another friend to see how her break went. Dani and Noah headed to the library to look at the newspaper archives before the bell rang.

"How do we find the story? What if they didn't report it to the press?" asked Noah.

"One question at a time, Noah. They would tell everyone if they made arrests and broke up the car theft gang. Remember, the Chicago Superintendent was trying to improve the department's reputation. The warehouse was on Claremont Ave, so let's start with that street."

The newspaper search returned several hits about building legal issues, real estate listings, and one article titled "Calamity on Claremont." Clicking on the link opened the article full screen on the library monitor. As Dani started reading, her chest tightened, and her heart felt like it had dropped into her stomach.

Police Sting Operation Turns Tragic as Officers Fall Victim to Violent Resistance

In a shocking turn of events, a police sting operation took a horrific twist last night when perpetrators brutally killed all officers. The coroner indicated the cause of death was due to the officers experiencing blunt force trauma on various parts of their bodies, leaving no survivors. Authorities remain baffled as they investigate this chilling and unexplained incident. The city was shocked at how an investigation into motor vehicle theft could turn deadly. Residents are concerned about their safety. More details to follow as the investigation unfolds.

"I think I'm going to be sick for real this time," Noah stated as he wiped the beads of sweat from his forehead.

Dani searched frantically for a follow-up article that brought closure to the tragedy, but nothing came up. It was clear the incident remained unsolved.

"We need to stop book-jumping. We're messing up the past." Noah said frantically.

"Seriously, Noah, how is this our fault? We have no idea how Kang became a phantom."

"Well, isn't it strange how he's been missing, and now he's inside our stories?"

"Sure, but we have always been alone when reading; it doesn't make sense."

"Doesn't matter," replied Noah, "we have to go see Mrs. Heks and get back into the story before the sting operation."

"... but how are we going to stop Kang? You don't even know what you are capable of."

"I have to try!"

The periods after lunch were agonizing for Dani. Her stomach still felt uneasy from their discovery, and she was starting to think it was also because she didn't eat anything for lunch. She was disappointed that she had let down her fellow officers and that Officer Hernandez was gone. She had just started her career in law enforcement, and her memories of possessing her were still fresh. She wanted to make a name for herself, not just to ride on her family's laurels from careers in criminal justice. Dani could relate to how different Emmy felt. Women officers only made up 22% of the Chicago police department, so they had to work extra hard not to be singled out as low-performers and sent to do the duties no one wanted.

Dani related to Emmy's feelings because she felt like a minority at her school. She didn't like wearing make-up or dresses and was not attracted to boys. Because she didn't follow the norm, kids would label her, and there were very few girls in the school like her. She considered how some girls were probably faking their appearance to fit in, but Dani was never a conformer. Dani decided long ago that being genuine was the least stressful. Having a few friends who liked her for her personality was better than a bunch of fake friends.

"Should we just walk downtown?" asked Noah when he met Dani in front of the school after the last bell rang.

"I guess so ... taking the bus, then biking there will take too long. Also, do you mind if I do the talking when we get there?"

"Why?"

"Because you embarrass me in front of her. You keep staring at her warts, and it's so obvious!"

"Sorry, I can't help it. Haven't you noticed? Every time we see her, she has more warts than the last time. Who gets that many warts so fast on their face?"

"Noah, just try not to go wart hunting this time, please?"

It took them about 35 minutes to reach downtown. The temperature dropped as they got closer to the ocean. The crisp, cool air kissed Dani's warm skin and revitalized her energy after the long walk.

"I'm parched. Can we grab a slushie at the convenience store?" Noah asked.

"For sure, I need to eat. Very little lunch and a long walk after school was not the best idea; I feel dizzy."

"What flavor do you want? Get some food; I'll get the drinks."

"Grape, if they have it, or cola, if they don't."

"Why not both?"

"Huh?"

"I'll layer them. I put all the flavors in mine, one on top of the other."

Dani looked confused, "What happens when they melt into each other? Wouldn't the flavor be kind of gross?"

"An expert slushie drinker like me won't let that happen."

"Just grape please, I'm not so adventurous with my food and drinks."

Noah insisted on paying for everything. It was the

least he could do after being taken on such a fun vacation. Barton's Books was only a short walk away, but Dani had easily consumed her hot dog by then. Although she experienced a twinge of guilt for indulging in junk food, the delightful signals emanating from her satisfied stomach squashed her dietary concerns. The door creaked as Noah pushed it open.

"Hello? Mrs. Heks, are you here?" Dani shouted as she walked further into the store.

The lights were lit dimly in the back of the store, and as usual, they were the only customers. Dani remembered Noah telling her that the books were not sold or loaned to customers with a tracking system like a library. Mrs. Heks would trust that people would read the books and return them. It seemed weird that people would not be lining up down the street for this free service. She called out a few more times, but there was no answer.

"Maybe she's busy or taking a dump; just be patient, Noah."

"Gross! ... Hey, the door to the office is cracked open," said Noah inquisitively. I can see some legs on the floor. Maybe she needs help. She's like, what, 100-something years old?"

"Have you ever seen someone over 80 years old, Noah? She's not in triple digits. Are the legs moving?"

"Nope, not for like the last five minutes."

"We haven't even been here two minutes!" Dani

leaned over the counter and directed her voice to the office door, "Mrs. Heks, is that you? It's Dani and Noah!"

There was no response, and the legs stayed rigid.

"Maybe she's taking a nap," said Noah. "Let's just go in there and make sure. We can't leave here without answers or a way to get back into that chapter. The guilt of our book trip is killing me."

Dani reluctantly let her legs pull her around the counter toward the entrance to the office. Noah followed behind her and grazed a seven-inch crystal dragon figurine on the counter. The bump tipped it over, and it headed toward the floor. Noah must have felt the brush because he swung around and scooped it up like he was catching a ground ball in baseball before it had a chance to shatter into pieces.

Dani flipped around, "What was that?"

"Nothing, thankfully!" Noah asserted, raising his eyebrows, which made his eyes appear bigger, paired with a soft smile.

Dani shook her head and turned back toward the office. Noah quietly replaced the dragon on the middle of the counter.

Dani didn't want to barge into the office, so she knocked on the door gently while pushing it open further. "Hello? Mrs. Heks?"

As the door opened wider, the body on the floor came

into full view. The figure startled Dani, and she jumped backward, smashing into Noah.

"Oh my God, Oh my God!"

Noah looked around Dani, "That's not Mrs. Heks."

"I know, I know ... I know ... I can't believe what I am seeing," Dani gasped.

"Who is it?"

Dani turned away from the woman lying on a thin mattress on the floor in the corner of the office. She looked at Noah, her eyes filling with tears.

"Remember the woman that owned one of the stores downtown, who had gone missing suddenly about a year ago? ... and they found her baby alone in the store as well as all her things, even her wallet and keys."

"Don't tell me that's her," replied Noah. Dani nodded slowly, raising her hands to cover her mouth in shock.

CHAPTER
TWELVE

THE DUO'S DILEMMA

Noah gently put his hands on Dani's shoulders to comfort her. He stepped around her into the room and moved closer to the still woman. From his experience as a firefighter, he checked her breath and pulse.

"Dani, she's alive. I think she's in a book coma like you were."

Dani rushed in and knelt next to Noah. "Thank you for checking. I thought she was dead. Dead people scare me. I had to attend my great aunt's open casket wake when I was probably, like, five years old. My mom made me go up to the coffin, and it really freaked me out. Ever since—"

"What is going on here?"

A cracking voice boomed behind a shelving unit filled with old wooden cartons. Noah looked toward the sound and noticed small vials of different shapes and sizes on one of the shelves. Some vials looked like they came from an ancient land; others appeared to have not moved in years from the thick, gray spider webs connecting them to the sides of the structure. Mrs. Heks emerged from behind the unit, and Noah quickly realized the office was much bigger than he initially thought.

"Shouldn't we be asking you that?" asked Dani as she stood up and pointed to the woman on the mattress.

"Child, she is fine, just in a perpetual slumber from her carelessness," replied the elderly woman as she began organizing some books on a nearby table. "This room is for employees only, and neither of you work here."

"You left the door ajar; we thought it was you on the floor and were concerned," Noah stated, trying to cover for their actions.

Dani was getting a little impatient with the misdirected conversation. "Mrs. Heks, you know the local police have been looking for Mrs. Tanner for almost a year now. How did you find her?"

"I know they have; I gave the police an anonymous tip about her baby after I found her 11 months ago in her store. I have told you before the books are my children. I always know where they are."

"So, you have had her here for that long? Why didn't you use the magic word and the book to bring her out of the story? Don't you know how important it is for a baby to have her mother?"

"Child, would you like some tea? You seem out of sorts. I use wild mushrooms in my tea; they are very calming."

Dani tried to be polite, but her voice started rising higher when she responded. "No! Thanks!" Noah noticed his friend's agitation and intervened.

"Mrs. Heks, we just want to know if we can help Mrs. Tanner as you have graciously helped us in the past."

"I tried using 'Endorshiftus,' but nothing happened. I then noticed the book had torn pages. The woman was careless. The magic that lives in the paper fibers was disturbed. There is really only one other way, but I don't think either of you will like it."

"Why?" replied Dani.

"I have run out of Chrono Amethyst Elixir. I might have enough for one more spell."

"Amethyst is a purple gemstone. Are you talking about the purple and silver potion you put on my finger before?" asked Dani.

"Precisely, Child. If we use it on Mrs. Tanner, you two

will never be able to go back into your story at a certain time again."

"You can't get more?" Dani questioned.

"These vials have been in my family for generations. I am sorry, my kind is a dying breed. Much of the craft knowledge has been lost."

Noah glanced at Dani with an uneasy look. That was precisely why they were there: to find a way back to the night of the disastrous police sting. As if he didn't have enough anxiety, now they had to make an impossible choice. Save Mrs. Tanner so her baby can grow up with a mother or save four officers from an evil phantom. Noah pulled Dani aside so Mrs. Heks could not hear them.

"May we have a moment, ma'am, to discuss?" asked Noah.

The spellcaster shuffled her feet to the back of the office near what appeared to be a small kitchen area. There was a strange stove half the height of regular stoves. Underneath a large vat danced a golden-red flame. It was the most giant pot Noah had ever seen. *How many people was she planning to feed?*

"I wish you had never shown me these books, Noah," said Dani.

"I'm sorry, but I'm glad you're here with me. I don't know how I could do this without you. Can we focus on the problem?" Dani nodded and started to bite down on her fingernail in deep thought.

Noah took another look at Mrs. Tanner. She seemed so peaceful. He noticed a tube coming from the back of her hand near the wall. He followed it up about three feet until he saw a plastic balloon-like bag hanging from a hook in the wall with a clear fluid inside. He remembered from his memories being Zach, the firefighter, that this was called an intravenous (IV) line and was used to feed nutrients to patients unable to consume food. Mrs. Heks kept the woman alive as if she were in a hospital.

"Isn't saving four people better than saving one?" asked Noah.

"That is an easy way to look at it, but have you considered that even if we can get back in the story, it doesn't mean we will successfully stop Kang? At least our chances of waking Mrs. Tanner seem much higher. Not to mention, her baby and maybe other people depend on her. Besides, police officers know the risks of their profession."

"Police officers have families that depend on them too!"

"You're right," sighed Dani, "What are we going to do? ... Wait, did you even bring the book? We don't have a fast way of getting home, and you know the spell only lasts an hour."

Noah removed his backpack and opened it on the floor. He pulled out the book and grinned at Dani.

"Mrs. Tanner is stable, Dani. I have an idea of how we

might be able to save her later, but let's work on one problem at a time. Who knows how many more people Kang will hurt or kill if we leave him to exist in the mystical realm," Noah insisted.

"Good point. He already has teamed up with one set of criminals." Dani called to the back of the office, "Mrs. Heks, we've made a decision!" She looked back at Noah. "Wait, what time is it?"

Noah came to the same realization that Dani probably had. Their parents were coming home from work soon, and they would worry that Dani and Noah were missing.

"We have to have the same story. What are we going to tell them?" inquired Noah.

"We're studying downtown and will eat here," replied Dani.

"Ugh!" grimaced Noah, "I hate lying to my dad, but I guess this is a life-or-death situation."

"Think of it this way: they'll be proud that we're already studying hard on our first day back at school."

"Sure, if my dad doesn't call my bluff. I'm not a straight-A student like you, Dani."

To Noah's surprise, his dad didn't question his actions after texting him. It probably was because he was working late that night. Returning from the holiday week was hectic for everyone.

They made their way to the back of the office, where they could use a couch to read. They didn't want to drop into a book spell with their bodies lying limber on the dusty, hard floor. Noah scanned the room, spotting a bathroom in the back corner as well as a coat and shoe rack. He realized Mrs. Heks lived and worked in the store. He felt a bit bad for her, but it quickly dissipated when he saw the soup boiling on the short stove. There were large pieces of bone floating around the bubbles, as well as what appeared to be beetles. Maybe his eyes were seeing things. He quickly turned toward the couch, which did not look alluring at all. The upholstery was a vibrant shade of avocado green, and it seemed like it had absorbed every stain, spill, and crumb that had come its way over the years. The cushions looked lumpier than the oatmeal he had for breakfast. The floor started to seem more inviting, and he swore never to complain to his dad about his old bed mattress again. He would have given anything to be back at home, reading in his room.

Dani opened the page in the blue book where she wanted to start and poked a small hole in her finger using a safety pin that she had seared on the stove flame. She wanted to avoid taking any chances with this trip by using her saliva on the page. Mrs. Heks sprinkled the silver dust on the pinprick and the rest of the purple elixir. The wound began to glow a purple-blue hue. As Dani touched the page with her enchanted finger, the book travelers faintly heard "Repee Expee Ditous."

CHAPTER
THIRTEEN

STING THAT STUNG

Officer Jones and Hernandez were driving to grab a bite to eat before meeting at the stakeout location for the police sting.

"Checkers sound good?" asked Officer Jones.

"I feel like we just had that," replied Officer Hernandez. Dani smiled internally, knowing it only felt that way because that's where they ate in the last version of this book trip. "I haven't had a home-cooked meal in ages. Can we stop by this Mexican food truck on Columbus and Western? It's on the way. They have the best tamales in the city, and their pollo is so juicy and tender."

"Maybe you should visit your poor old mother more often," responded her partner.

"I know, it's overdue. If I don't call her every other day, she calls the department looking for me. It's embarrassing."

"In her defense, you are a street cop in one of the most dangerous neighborhoods in Chicago."

"Yeah, Englewood's crime rate is only 276% higher than the national average," replied Emmy sarcastically.

"How do you acquire all these statistics?"

"Some of us know how to read," Emmy joked.

"You better be nice to me. I just gave up a mouth-watering burger for you!" cautioned Jim.

After grabbing their late dinner, they reached their assigned area near the warehouse on the northeast side of the Ashburn neighborhood. The rest of the officers were also in place scoping out the warehouse.

Noah remembered when the police bust went down shortly after 9 p.m. that night. As the time edged closer, he became more nervous. This was his one chance to make things right and save a bunch of lives. He still wasn't sure of the powers he had, but if Kang was strong enough to hurt people, he certainly could be strong enough to save them. The call came in to move in on the suspects. Officer Jones put their police vehicle in gear.

"Do me a favor and don't follow the SUV into the warehouse driveway," Dani told her partner.

"Why? The closer, the better to surround the suspects."

"Would you please trust me?"

Just then, they saw the garage door crash onto the police SUV. They slowed to a stop on the side of the curb just as the SUV was hurling backward. Office Jones' jaw dropped, and he looked over to Officer Hernandez.

"Holy crap! How did you know to stay back?"

"Women's instinct, I guess."

"Let's move!" roared Officer Jones. They exited the vehicle and drew their weapons while approaching the building.

Good luck, Noah; I know you can do it! Noah read Dani's mind as he slipped through the door gaps into the garage. He wouldn't risk Kang seeing him again, so he floated to the warehouse ceiling as high as possible. This also gave him a good visual of the perpetrators. He realized he had broken free from Dani, which he had never been able to do before. He also remembered when he was possessing a firefighter; his dad told him later that he couldn't move more than a few feet from Noah as a phantom. This was a great start, and he was already further into the story than the last time.

We have the building surrounded. Come out with your hands above your heads!

. . .

Noah heard the megaphone announcement from the officer in charge outside and watched as the carjackers scattered toward the two separate door entrances to the warehouse. He could see they were armed but not with anything too scary, just small handguns. Then he saw him. Kang followed behind the guy who was in charge. They moved toward the rear entrance just as a battering ram forcibly opened the door. The second officer through the door was Officer Hernandez.

Kang wasted no time jumping in front of Dani, revealing his frightening appearance. Emmy fired shots, but they were useless as they went through Kang's apparition, leaving a shiny silver-laded bullet trail as they flew across the room. Kang grabbed Emmy and flung her forcefully toward the front of the building.

"No!!!" shouted Noah.

Without even thinking, Noah swooped down as fast as he could. He enveloped her entire body with his purple and silver haze, then immediately converted his phantom body into a stiff cocoon-like structure. The momentum carrying Dani pushed them straight into the brick wall near the garage door. Noah barely felt the impact and converted back to a ghostly mist. Officer Hernandez's body gently slid through the fog and down the wall to the floor.

"Dani, are you okay?"

"I'm fine, thanks to you. Don't worry about me, get him!"

Upon observing the rescue, Kang's silver eyes turned bright red. Noah sensed he would try to phantom blast him to another universe, so he shot across the room. Expanding his phantom nebula allowed him to completely engulf the larger Kang before turning it into another hard cocoon. He concentrated hard to maintain his phantom jail for Kang as he watched the police apprehend the rest of the carjackers. He could feel Kang trying to free himself. The sound of police backup vehicles arriving could be heard outside. Dani was already on her feet and assisting one of the officers who was having trouble with one of the criminals. Noah watched proudly as Dani helped the other officers, one at a time. He couldn't believe the hand-to-hand combat skills she had acquired with her possession of Officer Hernandez. It was like watching a supercop fight scene on television. Moments later, he was distracted by Kang yelling inside of him.

"Let me out! I can't breathe!"

Noah thought about his situation. He could easily destroy Kang forever but didn't want to kill anyone. They may have saved the officers today, but Kang in his phantom form was capable of evil. He waited till he could feel Kang's struggle subside, and the officers were gone. Then he released his grip on Kang.

"I could have killed you," said Noah as he watched Kang cough, trying to recover from his asphyxiation.

"Why didn't you?" asked Kang in between coughs.

"A thank you would be nice. I wanted to talk to you and see if we can bring you back to our world. Don't you miss your family or being a kid?"

Kang laughed so loud and hard that it echoed around the large warehouse.

"... and give up all this power? Finding you twerps behind the school shed was the best thing that ever happened to me, except maybe you foolishly freeing me right now. See ya!"

To Noah's chagrin, he watched as Kang flew toward an open window. The silver and purple mist was sucked out swiftly like a gigantic vacuum was pulling him outside the building.

Noah found Dani outside the warehouse discussing the bust with the sergeant from their department, who assigned Dani and her partner the sting during roll-call earlier that morning. Noah was now, once again, invisible to everyone but Dani. Some officers inquired how Officer Hernandez had been thrown across the warehouse and survived. One thought there was some explosion because they saw enormous billows of smoke; other officers agreed but realized they were too busy apprehending the carjackers to be sure.

"You feeling alright?" asked the police sergeant.

"Yes, I couldn't be better, especially after this bust," replied Dani confidently.

"Promise me you'll stop by the hospital; you could have internal bleeding hitting that wall." The police sergeant started to walk away and turned his head back, "Oh, and terrific job in there, Hernandez."

CHAPTER

FOURTEEN

TEACHER'S PEST

As Dani's eyes regained focus, she immediately felt uncomfortable. Mrs. Heks stared intently at her while sitting on a small wooden stool, sipping her steaming soup. Dani noticed two terrible things. Usually, homemade soup smells warm and cozy, like a comforting hug on a cold day. Hers smelled like a combination of spoiled milk and burnt hair. Strangely, Mrs. Heks seemed to be enjoying every slurp. The second thing was how sore her lower back felt; it ached terribly. She observed Noah standing up slowly, grabbing his lower back with both hands. She realized the uncomfortable couch was the culprit.

"How long were we gone?" asked Noah.

"One turn of the hourglass, Child," responded Mrs. Heks.

Noah turned to Dani, shrugging his shoulders. "There's a reason they call it an hour ... glass, Noah," replied Dani.

"Oh duh!" Noah began to walk around the room to loosen his back up.

"I trust your journey was successful ... *CRUNCH!*" The sound from Mrs. Heks' mouth was disturbing. She reached into her mouth with her bony fingers and pulled out what appeared to be a black leg from a crawling creature that was stuck in her teeth.

Dani closed her eyes, trying to unsee what she had just seen. She looked toward Noah.

"I didn't see Kang after we locked the carjackers in our police vehicles. Did you destroy him?"

"I could have ... but I stupidly tried to reason with him."

"What! Why?" blurted Dani.

"I thought he might have missed his family and hoped we could help bring him back. Sorry, I'm not a killer!"

"—And when he finds the next set of criminals to work with, or even worse, just becomes a menace on his own?"

"I know, I know, Dani! The good news is he slipped up and gave me some information before he took off," smiled Noah.

"What do you mean?" replied Dani. Even Mrs. Heks was more interested in what Noah said than her putrid soup as she stopped eating for a few seconds and looked over, waiting for his response.

"Remember our trip into the firefighter book behind the school shed?"

"How could I forget the time you left me in a coma, which made my mom hysterical?" replied Dani.

Noah frowned but continued, "We wondered why we were firefighters, and there was no phantom. We were wrong."

"He was there! He became the Phantom!" exclaimed Dani.

"Yep, and that means—"

"The body is near the school's shed!"

Mrs. Heks cackled loudly. It was a bit frightening to Dani and Noah.

"So, I suppose you will want to borrow that book again, hmmm?" she asked.

"Yes, please, Mrs. Heks. We will bring it right back as soon as we use the spell to bring him back," replied Noah.

"Do you really think that's a good idea?"

Dani and Noah replied in unison, "Of course it is!"

"Is it?"

Mrs. Heks got up from her stool and slowly went to the sink to put her bowl inside. Dani was usually much more patient than Noah, but even this pause annoyed her. *What did she mean?*

With her back turned, she continued, "You remember your trips, correct? Is it really a good idea to bring a bad kid back who knows about these magical books?"

"What do you suggest?" said Dani.

"The Memerace spell."

"What's that?"

"I can only perform it, but it will wipe out any future memories from a specific time in the past," said Mrs. Heks.

"That's perfect! Will you come with us?" asked Noah.

"I am afraid not, Child. I am forbidden from performing magic outside of my home. The entranced boy must be brought here."

"Of course," sighed Noah, "anything to make this more difficult."

"I am getting tired now, and you must go! That comfy couch you are sitting on is calling my name. Would you two like some soup to take home?"

Dani rolled her eyes at Noah as she got up. "No, thank you, ma'am; we're headed to Belly Busters."

As they passed the potion shelf, Noah slipped the empty purple elixir bottle into his pocket without Mrs. Heks noticing.

"What are you doing?" Dani whispered harshly.

"Will tell you later, I have an idea," replied Noah.

Noah and Dani headed to Belly Busters. Dani still had some vacation money left over and wanted to treat Noah to a burger and dessert after his remarkable bravery while on their book trip. The comfort food smells tantalized their nostrils as they walked into the eatery. The owner directed them to Noah's favorite booth, which happened to be open.

"Are you thinking what I'm thinking about Kang's whereabouts?" asked Dani.

"The forest. It's the only place he could have gotten close enough to us and not be found."

"Yeah, but it's been weeks; how do we know his body is still there? For all we know, some coyotes could have gotten to him," Dani cringed at the gruesome thought.

"Last year, my dad and I saw a coyote munching on a deer in the middle of the road!"

"Noah, you are not helping!"

"You saw, Mrs. Tanner, she was being fed with fluids by Mrs. Heks. Kang has probably starved to death."

"Maybe the spell is preserving him."

"Possibly! Here is a better question," replied Noah, "Kang is the size and weight of a man; how are we going to get him back to Barton's Books? I mean ... I could drag him behind my bike; he deserves it."

"Noah!" Dani smacked him in the arm. "Another

question: why did you take the empty vial? If Mrs. Heks finds—"

"She won't! If she does, she may not care because it's empty. To answer your question, two words, Mister Boon."

"The science teacher?" Dani inquired.

"Yep! There has to be a small amount of that lixer—"

"E-lixir!"

"Whatever, you know what I mean. Mr. Boon could swab the inside of the vial and analyze it in the lab. Maybe he can tell us what it's made of so we can replicate it to save Mrs. Tanner."

"Noah, you've been watching too many cop shows, and I think that requires special equipment. I do like what you're thinking, though. How do you intend to get him to help you?"

"What do you mean?" Noah looked puzzled.

"You're the opposite of a teacher's pet. You always talk during lab time, never finish your projects, and don't clean up your space."

Noah handed the vial to Dani and grinned.

"Ugh," Dani grabbed the bottle, "Maybe you should buy *me* a burger."

Just then, their plates arrived. Dani was pretty impressed with Noah's favorite restaurant. The burgers were served on lightly toasted brioche buns with the letters "BB" branded on the top. The fries were crinkle-cut and golden with just the perfect amount of special seasoning. The cheeseburger was perfectly cooked and so juicy it was hard to stop eating once you started.

"Can I have your pickle?" asked Noah.

"Sure, there's no way I can finish even half of this burger. I've been meaning to ask you. How did you find your phantom powers?"

"Honestly, I just did what your mom told me to do." Noah took another big bite of his burger while stuffing three fries in with it.

"My mom? When did you talk to her?"

"Thaa nigh slepver," Noah answered with his mouth full. He swallowed and said "The morning after we got home from Cancun."

"My mom knows you were a phantom?"

"No, no, no, she mentioned something about following your feelings. I realized it's more important to act on your feelings than to wait for something or someone to tell you what to do. Even if your emotions steer you wrong, at least you learned something from that bad experience."

"Dang, Noah, all this time I thought that was empty," as Dani knocked on his skull, "Ha ha, guess I was wrong."

Noah shook his head and quickly stole Dani's last two fries.

～

Dani decided to try and catch Mr. Boon before the start of class the next day, so she asked her mom to drop her off at school a little earlier. Her friend, Kari, stopped her on the way to the science teacher's classroom.

"Dani, I need your help with something," said Kari. "I'm getting funny looks from other girls, and I think it's about my skirt. It's the first time I have worn it. It was, like, over 20 bucks at Aberteenie. If you tell me you don't like it, I'll return it."

"As you can probably tell, I don't have an eye for fashion," replied Dani.

"Just because you don't like wearing dresses doesn't mean you can't have an opinion. *Please!* I know you'll be honest with me; I don't trust those other girls.*"*

The conversation was boring Dani, but she wanted to be a supportive friend.

"The skirt is pretty, but maybe it's just a bit too short. Did you buy the wrong size?"

Dani was trying not to offend Kari, so she wanted to make it look like an honest mistake.

"I don't think so," replied Kari. "Thanks, BFF!"

Dani watched as Kari quickly made a beeline for the girl's restroom. She had heard Kari call several other girls "BFF" in the past, so she wondered what the "Best" meant in the nickname. The definition of "Best" was outperforming all others in a category, so to her, there could be only one. This was one of the reasons Dani didn't feel like she fit in at school.

Luckily, the conversation didn't take long, and she arrived at Mr. Boon's classroom with 10 minutes to spare before the first bell rang.

"Well, this is a nice surprise; how are you, young lady?" asked Mr. Boon upon seeing her.

"Terrific, sir. Could you help me figure something out? I have an idea for a future science project."

"You know I'm always interested in helping with my favorite part of the school year science curriculum; what did you have in mind?"

"Isn't there a way to analyze a substance to tell what it's made of?" asked Dani.

"You've been paying attention in class; *I love that!*"

"The device that analyzes samples is called a mass spectrometer. It's used to identify and quantify the chemical composition. Unfortunately, it's not in our school budget to have this special machine. We would have to send the sample to Cal up north."

"The university?" replied Dani.

"That's right. The University of California, Berkeley is one of the top research universities in the world, along with Harvard, Stanford, and MIT. I was fortunate enough to complete my Masters there."

"How long would that take?"

"We could get the sample there in a day, but not sure

how long it would take them to send us the results. I think the bigger issue is cost. Even with my alum discount, I think it would cost a couple hundred dollars. Do you have that kind of money?"

Dani was freaking out inside but tried to maintain her calm demeanor. "Yes, I can get that for you tomorrow. Can you get started getting the sample ready?"

"Absolutely. Do you have it?"

"Here you go."

Dani gave the vial to Mr. Boon, hoping he wouldn't ask any more questions given its strange appearance. Luckily, the bell was about to ring, so he was rushing to prepare for class. He took the vial and put it in his leather satchel bag.

As Dani walked briskly to her first period, she rummaged through her backpack's pocket for money. The feeling of multiple bills was encouraging until she counted it. Only $80 left from her vacation spending money. She hoped Noah had the rest. If not, she would have to ask Mom to pull from her birthday and Christmas savings, inviting many questions she wanted to avoid answering.

Dani and Noah met at lunchtime to try and inconspicuously find Kang's body near the maintenance shed.

"I'm nervous about this, Noah," said Dani as they walked toward the shed.

"Why?"

"What if he's dead ... or worse, we only find parts of him?"

"Let's just make sure he's there; you don't have to touch him. I will check him out," replied Noah.

They checked around to ensure nobody in the schoolyard saw them go inside the bushes behind the maintenance shed. They slowly moved to the forest side and pushed the bushes aside. Beyond the shrubbery was a small hill; the forest floor was lower than the school grounds. A human-like figure sprawled out at the bottom of the hill as if it fell and was now covered with leaves and dirt. They had found a body, but the only problem was it did not look like Kang.

FIFTEEN

BODY SNATCHER

N oah and Dani looked at each other with concern. They realized they would have to go down the small hill and inspect the body. Noah sensed that Dani wanted to stay as far away as possible, especially if it wasn't Kang. They slid down the leafy slope, careful not to get too much dirt on their clothes or accidentally slip on top of the seemingly inert form. Noah looked around the area and realized how easily someone could be lost there. The forest had trees of various trunk thicknesses with very dense branches that lost all their leaves in the early winter. Besides the lifeless figure, the area around them was a perfect setting for a scenic photograph. The wind howling around the trees made it feel a little spooky, and he watched as the breeze sent leaves flying in different directions.

"Here goes nothing," said Noah as he slipped his hand inside his jacket's sleeve.

He watched too many crime shows not to be careful. He didn't want to leave his fingerprints accidentally. If this wasn't Kang, the last thing he wanted was an investigator coming to their home. Using his sleeve, he swiped away the leaves that had gathered on the figure's face. *IT WAS KANG!* Noah was a bit surprised but also relieved.

"What the heck happened to him?" Noah asked.

Dani moved closer after realizing it was not a strange person. "He is half as big as he used to be!"

"He still has a pulse!" Noah continued to move away the brush that had gathered over the weeks on Kang. He noticed his chest rising and falling very slowly.

"We have to return soon; it's almost time for next period," replied Dani.

"Well, this is good news on two fronts," exclaimed Noah.

"Explain."

"We found him, and he is much skinnier. He'll be much easier to move."

"Good point. I think I know why ... the spell must have been using his body fat to feed him all these weeks so he could stay preserved. Didn't you notice how skinny Mrs. Tanner was? That was why she needed to be fed with an IV."

"Crazy! We better get going," said Noah.

"Wait! We can't leave him out in the open like this. Let's cover him back up!"

Noah and Dani quickly pushed the leaves on the ground back over the body to hide it as best as they could. As they did, Noah noticed Dani searching through Kang's jacket and eventually pulled something out of one of Kang's pockets. He was happy to see she was wearing gloves. They scampered quickly up the hill to get back to class.

After the last bell rang, the pair walked as fast as they could toward the bus waiting outside. They wanted to get to the bus early to grab the back seats for more privacy.

"Where did you get that from?" asked Noah.

Dani held up her index finger to pause Noah from talking as she counted the money in her hand. "... 146. I just need about 60 more dollars. "

"For what?"

"Mr. Boon said the sample needs to be sent to a university, which costs money."

"How much?" inquired Noah.

"Well, he thought about $200. I have $80 left from our vacation and just pulled another $66 from Kang."

"What! I was wondering what you grabbed earlier. I didn't know you were a Klepto?" sputtered Noah.

"First, I'm impressed you know what kleptomaniac is, and second, it's not stealing if it was already stolen. I can almost guarantee this is other kids' lunch money that Kang stole. Kang caused us to have to use the last of the elixir on him instead of Mrs. Tanner anyways, so he should help pay for it."

"Pretty sure it's still stealing," rebutted Noah. "In a way, you're right. Only *you, Danielle*, can make me feel good about something bad. I have some money left at home, for whatever else is needed, I can sell one or two of my older X-men comics. There's a store downtown that buys them."

"That would be fantastic. I don't want to ask my mom to go into my savings," replied Dani.

Noah looked around, and luckily, no one was sitting in the bus seat in front of them. He moved closer to Dani.

"How are we going to move Kang's body?" Noah whispered.

"I have an idea. My brother, Donny, owes me a favor after I didn't blab on him for taking my dad's Mustang out for a joy ride before he even got his driver's license."

"Does he have a license now?" asked Noah.

"Yeah, he does."

"Crap, that means we have to explain everything to

him. The more people that know, the less likely our secrets will stay discreet," worried Noah.

"Donny may be annoying sometimes, but he is the one person I trust completely. He has always had my back. He looks out for me. Once, when some random girls were teasing me at the mall for how I dressed, he put them in their place."

"How?"

"He was older than them, and when he approached the group, they started acting all flirty with him. To their surprise, he called them out for having no character or individuality like me, but instead, they were clones conforming to the latest fashion trends without any originality. Their facial expressions of embarrassment were priceless!"

"That's awesome, Dani!"

As Dani's stop neared, they agreed to text each other after dinner to give Dani time to talk to her brother. Noah watched Dani walk toward her street and couldn't help but wonder how he was so lucky to find such a great friend who was fun, intelligent, and supportive. He respected her individuality and wanted to gain the same level of trust as her brother had.

At 7 p.m., Noah's dad heard a monkey giggling in the bathroom. He turned the light on and answered Noah's phone.

"Noah's monkey business, how can I help you?"

"Oh, um ... excuse me, sir, this is Dani. Is Noah around?"

"Somewhere about, how are you doing?"

"Great! Still trying to adjust back to school life," replied Dani.

"I bet. Thank your mom again for taking Noah on your trip; he never stops talking about it. You ladies set the bar too high for me now!"

Dani laughed while Noah's dad called out to his son that he had a call. Noah rushed into the living room, and Mumu followed behind him like a shadow.

"Did you misplace something?" asked Noah's dad.

"Thanks, Pops!" Noah grabbed the phone and headed upstairs to his room.

Mumu followed until he reached the first step. Knowing his boundaries, he lay down, putting his head between his paws while releasing a big sigh.

"We have to leave now; my brother is on his way. Can you get ready?" urged Dani.

"Now? We were out late yesterday. My dad is not going to like me leaving again on a school night."

"We don't have a choice. I convinced my brother, but we have to do it tonight. His traveling baseball team is leaving tomorrow morning for a three-day tournament. He won't be back till the weekend. Besides, we can't leave Kang in fantasy land that long to do more damage."

Noah thought for a second, "It's Two-for-Tuesday!"

"Huh?"

"The movie theater has specials on Tuesday, where two people can go for the price of one. I'll tell my dad your brother is taking us there. Not a fan of lying, but this is important."

A backfiring exhaust rang out as Donny pulled up to Noah's house. Noah heard it from inside and went to the front door. Mumu followed; he was being extra clingy today for some reason.

"Sorry, Boy, you stay here and protect Dad. I'll be back soon."

As Noah approached the vehicle, it reminded him of one of those big dark-colored sedans you see on television, with the oversized trunk, four large doors, and non-descriptive black metal wheels. The engine growled as if waiting to do something sinister like transport a body.

"What's up, Phantom?" said Donny as Noah got in the back seat. "Sorry about the noise; I think my beast needs some new spark plugs."

Noah was a little surprised by the name he was called,

but Dani's brother either didn't believe a word Dani told him or was just one cool cat.

"Where did you pick up this ride? The interior looks much too new to be an older sedan."

"My dad and I got lucky. We found this baby on an online car forum. This older couple had kept it in their garage for like 20 years, hoping to give it to one of their grandkids. Their kids never had kids, so they sold it to me for about three grand."

"That's dope!" replied Noah.

They arrived at the school and noticed the gates were locked, so they stopped as close as possible to the school. As the car was put in Park, it backfired again, and Noah hoped no one heard it to start watching what they were about to do or, even worse, report a suspicious-looking vehicle. Luckily, it was nearly a full moon that night, making navigating the dimly lit yard more manageable. And Dani brought a large flashlight. They climbed over the fence and headed toward the shed.

As they got closer to the back of the shed, the flashlight reflected off two sets of eyes staring back at them. Noah remembered learning in biology that nocturnal creatures have tiny mirrors in their eyes that enhance their night vision. These mirrors make them glow when hit with direct light. It startled the three of them to the point where they stopped moving, but the animals quickly scattered into the night. Noah was happy and secretly hoped they were raccoons, not coyotes.

"He's down there," said Dani as she directed the flashlight below the bushes that lined the forest.

Donny stuck his head beyond the bushes and brought it quickly back.

"Where? I don't see anybody."

"Let me show you," replied Dani, motioning to Donny to look inside the forest again.

She peered down the eight-foot slope to the forest floor and shined her flashlight as Donny followed the beam. Noah got curious when the beam of light kept moving all over the place and stuck his head in just as he heard Dani yell.

"He's GONE!"

CHAPTER
SIXTEEN

COMIC PAIN

Dani started to tear up. Noah knew she was worried that they would never be able to stop Kang's phantom rage. They were the ones who put him in the alternate reality in the first place. Donny and Noah looked at each other and slipped down the hill to look around the forest. After about 10 minutes of looking in the dark, they gave up. The forest floor was a bed of leaves, leaving no trace of movement in any direction. They started to walk back toward the car.

"You guys are sure you saw him this afternoon?" asked Donny.

"Yes, we actually removed his leaf-covered face to confirm it was him!" asserted Dani. "He has been laying there for weeks, and as soon as we discover him, he vanishes in hours; it makes no sense!"

"Did anybody see you go to the back of the shed this afternoon? It's not like you were protected by the cover of night," asked Donny.

"We were very careful. We checked around before we went behind the shed and after. No one else knew, except ..."

Noah stopped talking and walking, falling a few paces behind the other two. Dani and Donny realized this and turned back toward Noah.

"Except what, Noah?" Dani questioned.

"She was there when we talked about our firefighter book trip," said Noah.

"Who?" asked Donny.

"Mrs. Heks ... " replied Noah, still trying to recall the point in their past conversation when the location of Kang was revealed.

"You're right. I remember distinctly how the slurping of that disgusting soup stopped while she must have been listening in on us. But that's impossible! She's too old and frail to move a body; she can barely move her own body!" stated Dani.

"You said it yourself; she's a witch; anything is possible with magic," replied Noah.

"But she said she is forbidden to use magic outside her home. This is so bizarre."

"Wait! Who is Mrs. Heks? A witch? You guys are mixed up in a fairy tale here, and I'm starting to think you both belong in the loony bin," exclaimed Donny.

Dani looked straight at Donny. "Trust us, you don't even know the half of it."

They got back to the car and decided to visit Barton's Books. It was late evening, but they couldn't return home without knowing what happened. Noah considered how Mrs. Heks might be sleeping by now, and their late visit would make her grumpier than usual. He was happy that Donny and Dani were with him in case the witch tried to harm them.

They parked away from the store and walked a short distance from the main street. Downtown Primrose Beach was like a ghost town this late at night; even Belly Buster's was dark inside. A winter wind picked up as they turned the corner toward the bookstore. It sent a chill down Noah's spine, only worsening his nervousness. They decided to leave Donny near the street when they rapped on the door. They didn't want to alarm the woman with a new face.

"We know she lives here; she has to be here," said Dani after waiting a few minutes for a response.

"Maybe she's a deep sleeper," replied Noah.

He tried to look through the stained-glass window, but

it was pitch black inside with no movement. He pushed the handle, but the door was locked. He knocked again. They looked back at Donny, who seemed impatient and shivering from the cold. Dani and Noah waited a few more minutes and started walking back to Donny; just then the door creaked open. They walked back, and the scent of burnt hair exited the bookstore.

"It's a little late to come by for my delicious soup," joked Mrs. Heks.

"We're sorry to bother you, ma'am" replied Dani.

"Do you have our classmate, Kang?" asked Noah.

"Why yes, isn't that what you wanted?" replied Mrs. Heks.

"But how were you able to get him here?" said Dani.

"I have little helpers, don't worry, Children. Come by tomorrow, and we can try the spell." The sorceress abruptly shut the door.

"Good night to you, too," jeered Noah.

"Let's just be thankful she has him; now we can sleep soundly," said Dani.

When Noah got home, he knew he had to do the unthinkable: sell one of his comics tomorrow. He pulled out his plastic bin loaded with cellophane-wrapped comics that he had been accruing since he started grade school. His dad was instrumental in forming his collection by providing him with the books he collected as a kid. He received one from his dad, called the "Uncanny X-men," where Gambit first appears. Noah knew it was worth something, even if it wasn't in perfect condition. He dreaded selling it, but they had to help Mrs. Tanner.

It was a rough start the following day at school. It was as if Dani's algebra teacher, Mrs. Mittins, wanted to see if her class was taking the return from winter break seriously. A pop quiz was on all the desks to test what they learned over the last two days. With Dani's extracurricular magic duties, she had yet to complete homework for the week. It was frustrating, but Dani powered through it the best she could. She met Noah at the bus stop after school; it was faster to take the bus to downtown than walk there.

Their trip to the comic bookstore was lucrative despite Noah having to give up one of his favorite possessions. The store owner appraised the X-men book at $95, which gave Noah more than enough to help Dani pay for the Berkeley lab work. On their way to Barton's Books, they passed the new arcade Noah's dad told him about.

"It's taking all my willpower not to go in there and spend the money in my pocket. *Look! They even have an arcade version of Triassic Traveler!*" exclaimed Noah.

"Sounds like I need to hold your money for you; hand it over," Dani put out her hand. "I just feel bad that these guys took over Mrs. Tanner's store."

"Vacant stores don't last long downtown; too many visitors to make money from," replied Noah.

Getting closer to the bookstore, Dani wondered about something. "What are we supposed to tell Kang once he wakes up?"

"I didn't think that far ahead, but didn't she say his memory will be zapped? He might not even know who we are."

"Does it matter? If I woke up in that back room, I would be scared. Heck, I'm scared to go back there, even now. It's dimly lit, smells bad, has an unconscious woman lying on the floor, and then, of course, you know who," said Dani.

"We'll think of something; let's just hope her spell works," said Noah.

As they walked up to the bookstore's entrance, a young boy and his mother were leaving. The boy seemed excited about the vintage-looking book he was carrying. Dani desperately wanted to warn them, but where would she even start? "*Hey strangers, don't spit or drip blood in that book ... oh ... and one of you might become a scary-looking powerful phantom.*" They would either bust out laughing or run as fast as they could in the other direction. Besides, every book can't be magical.

"Please lock the door behind you," requested Mrs. Heks, seeing the duo walk in.

"Oh ... right," said Noah, turning back to the door. "Where is he?"

Mrs. Heks gracefully motioned the two to follow her with her thin, bony fingers. Dani walked behind her and couldn't help but notice how long her nails were. They weren't like that yesterday. It was creepy but not as bad as the visual of two bodies lying on her office floor. Kang was in the middle of the floor, entirely outlined by burning candles. Tiny red gemstones were lying on his face.

"Why are those there?" Noah pointed to the stones.

"One for each week you want to erase. Did I get it right?" replied Mrs. Heks.

Dani immediately tried to calculate how many weeks were in Kang's life. She wished she could erase his memory back to when he first decided to be a bully. For now, the last several weeks would do. She watched as Mrs. Heks laid the glowing *Fearless Firefighter* book on Kang's stomach.

"Kneel on both sides of him," ordered Mrs. Heks, "we need you both close to help pull him out. He has been in the story too long and has now connected with other books."

The witch kneeled by Kang's head and opened a glass jar wrapped in cobwebs. She started to drink its contents. The taste seemed to disagree with her, but she still swallowed it forcefully. She leaned her head over Kang's and grabbed his mouth with claw-like fingers. She appeared to be preparing to kiss him, but instead, Dani watched in horror as a sizable silver-colored worm squirmed slowly from her mouth and into Kang's. She whispered several words before suddenly pulling her head away from Kang. She closed her eyes and formed a prayer pose with her hands.

The red book started glowing brighter and brighter, like a thousand candles burning in one spot. Dani feared it was on fire. Strangely, there was no increase in temperature around the book. Kang's body started convulsing wildly. Dani and Noah locked on each other's frightened eyes until suddenly ...

WHOOSH!

CHAPTER
SEVENTEEN

WHO'S KANG?

A grayish-purple cloud of air emanated quickly from the book and blasted out in all direc- tions. It immediately extinguished every candle around Kang and was so forceful that it sent the kids and Mrs. Heks flying onto their backs. Noah could hear items crashing to the floor as the pressurized air swept around the room like a miniature tornado had touched down inside the bookstore's office. Kang's body stopped moving, and he began to sit up with his eyes still partially closed. Noah reacted quickly and threw a burlap sack over Kang's head. He then grabbed the red book and swiftly swung it with an uppercut motion to Kang's chin. Kang's head fell back like a sack of potatoes.

"Oh my God! What are you doing, Noah?" yelled Dani.

"Insurance plan," replied Noah.

"Huh?"

"Heard it on a cop show once; it's like a backup plan in case our original plan fails."

"What! If you were going to try and kill him, why did we even bother with the first plan?" fumed Dani.

"He's fine. I just knocked him out like he was in a boxing ring."

Mrs. Heks checked Kang's pulse and snickered, finding humor in Noah's actions. "He's of the living, children."

"I still don't get it," said Dani, "the whole point of this was to send Kang's memory back so he wouldn't remember anything."

"Sure, and what happens when he looks around and sees us, not to mention this room that looks like a *Harry Potter* movie set," replied Noah.

"What is *Harry Potter*?" asked Mrs. Heks. Dani and Noah looked at each other and wondered where this woman's been.

"You're right, I guess," said Dani. "But we could have figured out something else besides violence. I can't think of anything right now, to be fair. Where did you get that burlap sack, anyways?"

"I found it by the stove earlier."

"I use that to collect my earth creatures for my broths. You know, like worms, cockroaches, and beetles. The oriental cockroaches are actually quite sweet tasting,"said Mrs. Heks.

"Geez, Noah, I hope the bag was empty," Dani said, cringing. "Okay, now what do we do with him?"

"Can you call your brother to pick us up?" asked Noah.

"No, remember, he's on his way to his baseball tournament."

While the two were thinking about what to do, Mrs. Heks headed to the corner of the room and into the bathroom. They started to hear strange noises like she was regurgitating, but it did not sound like it was coming from a frail older woman. The retching was deep as if it was coming from the belly of a large animal, and the splashing sounds reverberated off the thin wooden door like bowling balls being dropped in the toilet.

"Can we please get out of here now?" Noah said with his hands in a pleading prayer form.

Dani and Noah put Kang's floppy arms around each of their shoulders to drag him toward the bookstore entrance. Noah was happy that he was so thin now; even with his height, he probably weighed less than Noah.

"Wait, let's take off the sack; we can't walk out in broad daylight with a kid wearing a bag over his head!" said Dani.

Luckily, it was already dark outside when they left the bookstore. Noah found one of his baseball caps in his backpack and put it over Kang's head to conceal his closed eyes better. There wasn't anyone walking around, but just then, a car zipped by from behind them on the street. Their nerves frayed, and instinctively, both pretended like they were laughing with Kang while huddling together in a circle. A bus stop was nearby with a bench enclosed by a semi-transparent transit shelter to protect waiting passengers from the elements. They decided to leave Kang there. They propped him up on the bench seat the best they could.

"One more thing left to do," said Dani as they briskly walked from the bus stop. Noah's head was on a swivel as he kept looking in multiple directions for witnesses.

"What's that? Haven't we done enough for one afternoon?"

Dani pulled out the missing person flyer from their school bulletin board and showed it to Noah.

Downtown Primrose Beach had one of the last existing working payphones on the planet. Dani dialed the number on the flyer while Noah's head swiveled around continually. Dani held a small box to the phone speaker as she heard an answer.

"I have some information on the missing boy," said a robotic voice with a scratchy skipping undertone.

Noah watched Dani in shock as she provided the location of Kang through the voice box.

"Where did you learn to do that?" he asked as she hung up.

"You're not the only one who watches cop shows!"

The entire Primrose Beach police department appeared at the main street corner. Kang was awake on the bench, gently touching his red and purple chin. A few officers approached him with one of their hands on their unsnapped gun holster.

"Son, are you alright?" asked Officer Trent.

"Umm, I think so," replied Kang.

"Are you Kang?"

"Who's Kang?"

The officer provided an update on his police radio strapped to his shoulder. He looked back over at Kang.

"You're not Kang Butte?"

The boy on the bench thought hard momentarily, then smiled, "My name is Harry Butte. Lots of people think it is 'butt,' but it's pronounced like 'beaut.' No one in my family has the name Kang, at least not that I know of."

"Son, do you know where you are and what day it is?" asked the officer.

Looking around, Kang responded, "Well, looks like I am downtown, and I'm sorry my head hurts a little, so I'm not sure what exact day it is. I do know Christmas is coming soon."

"I hate to break it to you, Son, but we are already into January. You have been gone for weeks."

"What? Where are my mom and dad?"

"On their way," the officer assured him. "We also have a paramedic coming; we should get you to the hospital to get your head checked."

Harry felt outstanding except for a very sore chin. He started to wonder what had happened. The last thing he remembered was coming downtown with his mom to shop for a Christmas present for his dad. He felt famished and kept inspecting his body. *Why am I so skinny?*

"Are you sure you're not injured?" asked Officer Trent, observing Harry move his hands over his body.

"No, I feel great!" Harry remembered being very over-weight and was trying to contain his excitement about his newfound slim form.

Harry's parents arrived just then and ran over to him, squishing him with a hug like he was a piece of ham, and they were the slices of bread in a deli sandwich. He couldn't remember the last time his parents hugged him, not even on his birthday this past summer.

"Let me look at you, Son," said his mom. "We were worried sick—"

"And we feared the worst," said his dad.

Harry felt like everyone was looking him over with disbelief, as if he just arrived from another planet. The attention felt good, especially from his parents. The paramedics arrived and ran some preliminary checks on Harry. Besides the minor contusion on his chin, he checked out fine. His parents convinced the officers to let them take him to the hospital tomorrow because they wanted to spend time with their son. Comfort food was the right choice, and the happy family headed to Belly Busters. After ordering a country-fried steak and mashed potatoes, Harry decided against dessert now that he had a second chance to eat better and live healthier.

"I'm surprised you didn't order two cokes, like usual," inquired his mom.

"Do you know how much sugar is in those, Mom?"

She took his hand between hers, her eyes tearing up, "It is so good to have you back."

Harry smiled widely, "It's great to be back; I feel like a new person!"

CHAPTER
EIGHTEEN

GOOD RUMOR

Dani and Noah worked hard to catch up on their actual lives before the weekend. They were itching to jump back into the blue book story, but their evenings of rescuing Kang took a toll on their schoolwork. It was amazing to see the story of their lost classmate make national news; it was also all over the internet. One of the local television stations even played the anonymous tip call that Dani made in her modified techno-voice. Dani giggled to herself when she heard it. By Friday's lunchtime, a rumor was going around the school about Kang, who was already back in class. Only it wasn't Kang; he was going by Harry now and was different —but good different.

"This totally makes sense now," said Dani as she took a bite of the food from her lunch thermos.

"What does?" asked Noah, grabbing a potato chip from Dani's bag.

"Wouldn't you change your first name if your real name sounded like Hairy Butt?"

Noah suddenly spit out some chip pieces at Dani as he cracked up.

"Eww!" gasped Dani, "You could have turned your head!"

"Sorry!" replied Noah. "That is so true, but have you heard the bigger news today?"

"No, I've had a busy morning. I gave the money to Mr. Boon, who was nice enough to front the payment for us and already sent the sample. He showed me the tracking information on his computer; we should have an answer early next week. "

"Awesome!" exclaimed Noah. He leaned closer to Dani to whisper. "I heard that he's not bullying people anymore, and at the earlier lunch period, someone actually saw him eating a salad."

"A salad? Who does that? Only rabbits, right?" Dani jested.

"Okay, funny girl, but when he used to eat his lunch, it

was typically a burger from the cafeteria, and then off to steal one or two other kids' lunches!"

"Noah, you care way too much about Harry's diet. We did good. I'm happy to hear he's treating people fairly. Let's see how long that lasts, though."

"We did do good!" Noah and Dani high-fived each other. "So, can you hang tonight with a certain Officer Emmy Hernandez?" asked Noah.

"Shoot!" My mom was super explicit this morning; she probably told me like four times. "*Come home right from school; we have work to do that you missed out on this week,*" Dani impersonated her mom.

"That sucks! How about tomorrow?" asked Noah.

"Once I finish being enslaved tonight, she'll be in a better mood for me to ask. "

That Friday feeling went completely away the second Dani walked into her house that afternoon. Her mom was hustling about mopping the floor, the vacuum stood upright in the living room, a garbage bag was lying open in the middle of the kitchen, and Dani barely got a "Hello, how was school?" out of her. Dani wondered briefly what it was like for her brother, Donny, who lived with her dad. Her jealousy quickly diminished after remembering a visit three weeks ago where she went to use the bathroom and ended up putting toilet paper on the seat before sitting down, just like it was a public restroom. She loved a clean house, like her mom, but her mom was a bit of a clean freak.

"How can I help?" Dani said, hoping her mom would tell her to have a snack after a long day at school first. NOPE!

"The living room needs vacuuming, and don't forget to move the couch to get under it, too," replied Dani's mom.

Who moves the couch every time they vacuum?

They had one of those newer vacuums that shows all the dirt swirling around as it collects from the floor. To satisfy her curiosity, Dani checked, using her fingers as a measuring device, how much dirt was in the clear container. It measured two fingers thick from the last time they cleaned the house. She went about her chore, vacuuming what appeared to be a spotless carpet. Moving the couches and the heavy, iron-casted dining room chairs was a workout. Her mom preferred an old-world look. The chairs were dark bronze in tone with a back with a metal swirl design underneath a cherry wooden cap. The cushions were foam-covered with a burgundy designer fabric that looked like it came from the 19th century. Dani could not understand why they needed a table with eight of these heavy chairs when there were only two of them. They never ate in the dining room and rarely had anybody over.

It took her almost three hours to complete all her chores, including the bathrooms. She heard her mom making dinner. She placed the vacuum back into the utility closet. She rechecked it, *still two fingers, maybe even less, after vacuuming the whole house!* Dani sighed as she walked into the kitchen, desperately wanting to tell her mom about her little vacuum experiment but also knew it would only start an argument.

"Relax, Honey, dinner is almost ready."

"Thanks, Mom."

Dani grabbed a tall glass of ice-cold water from the dispenser on the refrigerator and planted her behind hard into the seat at the kitchen table while pulling out her phone. She noticed the table wasn't set and was surprised her mom didn't ask her to do it, but she was tired and just wanted to catch up on her mobile feeds.

"Lost Beach Boy Interviewed by Popular YouTube Influencer" was the first story she saw when accessing her FastGram app. She hoped the magic wasn't temporary, and Harry suddenly remembered everything, like what happens when someone has transient amnesia. She knew his fame would fade as soon as the media was distracted by a new story that would sell more advertising.

"Hope you're hungry," said Dani's mom, "Thought we would try this air-fried salmon and pea couscous."

She placed a plate down in front of Dani. A perfectly cooked steaming filet of juicy salmon sat on top of a bed of tiny yellow balls mixed with green peas and orange carrot bits. Couscous has a rice-like appearance but is pasta.

"Looks amazing, Mom!"

"Let's hope it tastes as good as it looks."

The salmon melted in Dani's mouth and was perfectly seasoned with a tangy teriyaki dressing. Dani was hungry after the long day and wondered if food always tastes better when you are hungry. It's as if your taste buds are so bored waiting for food that they get as excited as a kid at a surprise birthday party when it comes. With her stomach satisfied, she thought it was a good time to ask her mom about something bothering her for several weeks.

"Mom, can I talk to you about something?"

"Of course, Baby, what's on your mind?"

"Why don't you take me shopping for clothes like other girls' moms do at school?"

Dani's mom looked a little surprised by the question; she finished chewing quickly and forced a swallow.

"Honey, you like to wear your brother's old clothes."

"Yeah, but I wouldn't mind having something new once in a while. It doesn't even have to be new; there are two vintage stores downtown that have some gently used designer clothes."

"Oh, umm, I never knew—"

"Well, you also never asked. Are you embarrassed by how I like to dress, Mom?"

"No, I just don't understand it. Sorry, I guess ... I guess I'm old school," explained Dani's mom.

"I have it hard enough with people I don't know, accepting how I identify. I could use some support from my family. Dad seems to understand just fine."

"You're right, Honey. I love you, and I've been selfish. I haven't been thinking about how you feel first. Come here."

Dani's mom stretched out her arms. Dani leaned in and hugged her. It was one of those genuine hugs that lasted a while, unlike the ones they had when she was leaving for school. The embrace and talk warmed Dani's heart, and it was a perfect complement to the yummy dinner.

"How about we go downtown tomorrow and look around?" asked Dani's mom.

"Can we make it Sunday instead? Noah and I were thinking of hanging out for a while."

"Of course, Dear. Can you help me with the dishes?"

"How about you find a romantic comedy on Netflix for us? I got the dishes," said Dani, smiling while putting her mom's plate on top of hers.

CHAPTER
NINETEEN

AN ACT OF VALOR

The bed covers masked the winter chill in her bedroom. Dani usually left the window cracked to keep her room cool at night, but she had failed the night before to check the weather report for Saturday. A cold front had swept over Primrose Beach in less than eight hours, bringing a downpour of rain and unseasonably low temperatures. The open window magnified the sound of rain tapping against the outside metal sill in a continuous pattern. This caused Dani to wake up worried, thinking her room was flooding. One turn to look at the window abated all concern, and she was too tired to get out of the warm bed to close the window. She tried to drift back into dreamland, but her phone's ringing annoyed her from the nightstand.

"Are you coming over?" asked Noah.

"Who is this?" responded Dani, lowering her voice.

"Uh, duh, you know!"

"No, I don't; sorry, you have the wrong number."

There was a brief moment of silence on the other end of the phone and the sound of fidgeting till Dani heard a short sigh.

"Gotcha! You had to look at your phone and check, didn't you?" Dani laughed.

"Yeah, yeah ... anyways, my dad got some sort of stomach bug from eating leftovers that were in our fridge for over a week. I told him not to do it, but he did anyway. He's glued to the bathroom. Want to hang out? I can make a fire in the fireplace. We can play games, or you know what."

"Sounds good, just waking up; give me an hour or so."

Noah tried to make a quick pass around the house to get it cleaned up, but his bedroom was in shambles. Thankfully, he had some time and, with it, found the dirty underwear under his bed before anyone else did. It was impossible to know how long they had been lying there.

He also got the quick start fire log ready. His dad didn't allow him to burn natural wood as it was a little unpredictable with how it broke apart, especially when it snapped from the intense heat. The fire logs were a set and forget-it luxury. They were wrapped in combustible paper that had to be lighted on both ends, which started the fake log inside. The logs burned slowly and consistently. His dad had even purchased the special logs that crackled like a real fire while they burned.

Mumu perked up his ears, then raised his head while resting near the fire and quickly moved to the front door. He used to bark when Dani came over, but he was accustomed to her now, and his tail wagged excitedly when he saw her in the window.

"Hey, cutie," said Dani as she walked in. She started rubbing her two hands up and down Mumu's neck.

"Oh, I thought you were talking to me," Noah said, smiling.

"Ha, you wish!"

"Let me put your coat somewhere to dry. Can't believe it's still raining hard. Head to the kitchen and tell me what flavor you want."

"Flavor?"

"Hot chocolate, I have a special machine that makes all different types,"

"Cool, seems like a perfect day for having that."

It wasn't long before they heard the word "Plasmador"

whispered, and they were teleported to the 7th District in Chicago. They dropped in right after the morning's roll call, and Officer Hernandez couldn't help but notice how everyone was greeting her by name. She only worked closely with a handful of the officers in the department. *What is going on, Noah? What did we miss?*

"Officer Hernandez!" Dani turned around.

"Yes, Commander, how are you?"

"Nice to see you back; I trust the time off after the raid did you some good."

"Absolutely," Dani did feel entirely rested in Emmy's body, which wasn't usually the case with the late work shifts.

"First Deputy Superintendent Racino is waiting in my office for you."

"Wait ... I thought I heard you say Supt. Racino is here," replied Dani.

"I did. Do you want to keep him waiting longer? Let's go."

"Who is that?" whispered Noah while his phantom form glided unsuspectedly over a busy hallway of officers.

He is second in command, reporting directly to the Superintendent of the entire Chicago Police Department!

As Dani walked into the Commander's office, she was greeted by the Deputy Superintendent and the Commander from the neighboring 8th District.

"Please sit down, Officer Hernandez," said Supt. Racino, "We wanted to let you know that we reviewed the bodycam footage from the police raid at the warehouse on Claremont."

Oh crap, did they see the Phantoms? How am I going to explain—

"It was difficult to make out some things with the explosions and gases fogging up the room, but your bravery was super clear even if your bodycam broke when you were thrown," the Superintendent went on saying.

Oh my gosh, I forgot to turn it on again!

Hearing Dani's thoughts, "That's a good thing, for the Phantom's sake," whispered Noah.

"Not sure what to say, sir. I was just doing my job," remarked Dani.

"Well ... no one can tell me how you were able to get up after being thrown across the room with that blast. Then you helped the other officers apprehend the perpetrators even after one was unarmed by one of the carjackers."

Dani tried to think quickly, "Tires, sir."

The deputy superintendent looked at her as if he didn't understand what she said.

"I believe I fell into a pile of rubber tire scraps, sir." Dani wanted to diffuse any more investigation into her incredible feat.

"So, you are not only fearless but also fortunate,"

smiled Supt. Racino. He slid a box across the desk. It was covered in red velvet and looked like those someone might pick up in jewelry stores. He propped the box open and extended his hand, saying, "Congratulations Hernandez!"

Dani couldn't believe what she was staring at. It was the Superintendent's Award of Valor. The box neatly displayed an antique brass medal inscribed with "Chicago Police" and the word "Valor." The medal hung from a nylon ribbon with two red vertical stripes bordering a white center stripe. Above the award was an additional smaller rectangular ribbon with the same striping and edged all around by gold stitching. Dani realized that the Superintendent's hand had been extended for an awkward length of time.

"Sorry, sir, I'm just a little shocked." Dani shook his hand happily. "Thank you so much!" The rest of the department staff in the room clapped, and Dani could hear Noah whistling into her ear as well.

"We don't just give those out to anyone, you know," said Supt. Racino, "But you deserve it, and I have some other good news."

Dani stopped staring at the medal and looked back up at the Superintendent.

"The CPD is also nominating you for the Medal of Valor, which, as you may know, is presented by the President!"

"What? I can't say how honored I am, sir. Thank you so much again." Dani was beaming inside but tried to maintain her composure. She knew not even her highly decorated late father had ever been nominated for that prestigious award."

"Just keep in mind, you will have a lot of competition. Nominations come in from police departments all over America, but only a handful win. It is the highest award a public safety officer can receive." said Supt. Racino.

"I will keep that in mind, sir," beamed Dani.

"Now get back to work, officer. The streets are safer when you're out there, not sitting in here."

Dani got up from her chair, grabbed the red box on the desk, nodded to her Commander, turned around, and walked out of the office with the broadest smile that the skin of her face would allow.

As she walked to her locker, she realized how lucky she was and now knew why everyone knew her in the department. They probably heard rumors she was being considered for the Presidential award while she took some time off. All of that didn't matter. Dani could feel Emmy's proud feelings and the longing to have her father there to tell him. Somewhere in the afterlife, her dad was smiling too.

"We did it again!" said Noah after they were alone in the locker room.

"Yep, I couldn't have done this without your phantom help."

"That's not what I'm talking about," replied Noah. "We changed this officer's life for the better. I'm ashamed to admit it, but I read ahead in the book. Don't worry, I was super careful. I wore a mask and heavy-duty gloves from my dad's workshop."

"Are you saying this wasn't part of Emmy's past?"

"Yep, she never mentioned this medal or the nomination. She did win a few other ribbon awards. It's as if the rest of the book becomes fiction now instead of nonfiction."

"Interesting way to look at it, Noah. I'm glad we made her life better."

"You want to know something else that I just realized?" Noah exclaimed.

"That you are a boy hanging around inside a women's locker room?" smirked Dani.

It was the first time Dani saw fear in the typically formidable face of the phantom. Noah's ghostly head swiveled quickly from the left to the right.

"Dani, you tricked me. Is anyone here?"

"No, don't you think I would have thought of that already?" replied Dani. "Now, what were you saying?"

Noah sighed and recollected his thoughts, "Oh yeah, did you know that a police badge is also called a shield?"

"No, but that makes sense; a shield shape symbolizes protection," said Dani.

"And ..."

"Noah, I can't read your mind; I'm not even sure you have a mind in that purple smoke-filled head."

"Are you sure you want to make fun of the phantom now that I have powers? But that's what I'm talking about. We couldn't figure out the phantom's powers, but now I know what they can be. Twice, I protected you with what?"

"A body shield!" responded Dani.

"Right! The phantom super enhances the skills of the body it follows. Police officers protect and serve. I wish I had figured this out earlier. Can you imagine what we could have done as firefighters? Who knows? Maybe I could have made it rain on fires!"

"The possibilities are endless—"

As Dani spoke, their bodies were transferred back to a chilly living room where the cozy fire had long since burned out. Mumu got tired of waiting and fell asleep between them, curled up in a ball on the floor.

CHAPTER

TWENTY

ELEMENTAL

Monday was a lot more exciting for Dani and Noah than usual. Usually, they dreaded starting a new week of school, especially now that the winter weather was getting colder and blusterier. The comforts of home made them miss the pandemic homeschooling. Today was different because they were getting the results of the laboratory sample analysis. The weekend they had left them both feeling great about themselves. Not only did they help send Officer Hernandez on a better career path, but both of them also spent some quality time with their parents on

Sunday. Dani's mom took her shopping, which resulted in a new outfit for Monday. She wore an oversized button-down short-sleeve shirt Noah would typically wear, baggy track pants with a green stripe down the side that matched her top, and brand-new white sneakers. Noah's dad finally recovered from his food poisoning, so they played a marathon of video games, including three hours of an MLB title, which resulted in finishing an entire baseball season in one afternoon.

"I told Mr. Boon we would be there right after school to review the report. Don't be late." Dani told Noah while they walked down the halls toward their first-period class.

"What if there's some ingredient they can't recognize, like it came from another planet?" asked Noah.

"Seriously, Noah, sometimes I think you watch too many science fiction movies. Witches are not from other planets; as a matter of fact, they leverage the Earth's treasures and creatures to make their potions. For example, in Shakespeare's 'Macbeth,' they describe a concoction that consists of the 'toe of frog, wool of bat and tongue of dog.'"

"You are not taking Mumu's tongue!!" exclaimed Noah.

"Relax, the names are not to be taken literally, usually. For example, in the old days, the wool of bat was just an old-world name for holly leaves."

"That's a relief," sighed Noah.

As Noah entered the classroom, his mind focused on school, and panic slightly set in. He still needed to finish his life science homework that was due today. Usually, his next thought would be, *Why do I need life science anyway? It's not like I'm going to become a scientist. I need to get better at baseball and play that for a living.* That thought started to creep into his head when he realized he should start learning this stuff. *I'm about to create an earthly potion with my best friend to save another human, hopefully.*

When Noah and Dani walked in, Mr. Boon was cleaning some test tubes in the sink with a nylon-bristled brush. He smiled when he saw the kids, and they exchanged pleasantries.

"Are you here to turn in your late homework, Noah?" asked Mr. Boon.

Noah looked over at Dani, embarrassed that she now knows, "I promise to tomorrow, sir."

"You sent me an email yesterday that you heard back from Berkeley," said Dani.

"Oh, right! Let's head to my office. It's on my computer there."

Noah waited patiently as the old computer fired up. He wondered why schools always seemed to have the most ancient equipment. He then remembered his dad saying that public school was free. Sending Noah to a private school would cost his dad too much money. That's probably why they were always doing fundraisers, like when he had to sell Christmas wrapping paper to his neighbors one year. He wished some of the wrapping paper money went toward Mr. Boon's limping computer.

"Here we go, opening now," said Mr. Boon. The email opened with the sample composition. It was only four ingredients, but it might as well have been written in Chinese because Noah had no clue what they were.

Sample 14587 contains:
  1) 5 mg Terpinen-4-ol
  2) 3 mg Datura Stramonium
  3) 1 mg Capsaicin
  4) 2 mg Cinnamaldehyde

"At least there are only four," said Dani. "The fourth one is just cinnamon, right?"

"Nice job, Dani. The third one is what gives things like chili peppers their heat. The first one comes from lavender, I think. That's probably what gives the substance its purple color. I need to look up the second one." replied Mr. Boon.

Mr. Boon searched the internet for the second substance. It turns out its common name was Jimson weed. It's a weed that grows in North America and is toxic when ingested due to the alkaloids it contains.

"Oh, that sounds dangerous," replied Noah. "What are alkaloids?"

"Alkaloids have alkaline properties which can provide anything from medicinal to psychoactive effects on people. Some bad drugs are alkaloids, but so is caffeine," answered Mr. Boon. "Where did you get his sample, anyways? And what do you plan to do with it?"

Noah and Dani looked at each other, wondering who should answer. Noah stalled because he couldn't think of anything but Barton's Books, which he didn't want to say.

"My grandma, sir," replied Dani. "You know, these older folks always think they have found the fountain of youth. She puts this on her wrinkles or something and couldn't remember where she got it." Noah was impressed by Dani's witty response.

"Well, she better wash her hands after applying; even the smallest amount of Jimson ingested can be toxic," said Mr. Boon.

"I think we can find the other three, but where can we find the weed?" asked Dani.

"No clue, says here; sometimes it's even found on the side of the road."

"Mr. Boon, can you print that report out? We really appreciate your help," said Noah.

"Of course, kids, but wait ... Dani, I thought you said you were using this for your upcoming science project."

Noah froze, wondering how they would respond to keep Mr. Boon from getting more suspicious.

"It's a project on alkaloids, of course ... " said Dani.

Mr. Boon smiled as he handed Noah the printout, "Great, enjoy finding your elementals!"

"Huh?" said Noah.

"Having the power of a force of nature, Noah," replied Mr. Boon.

Noah suddenly had more interest in science. Mr. Boon was brilliant and just helped them with a real-world problem. He motioned to Dani for them to go; they had work to do.

They were able to grab the last bus leaving for the day and made their way downtown. The two headed to the supermarket, hoping to find at least three ingredients. They couldn't find the lavender but headed to the checkout line with sticks of cinnamon and a few organic red chili peppers. While waiting for the customer in front of him, Noah glanced at the cover story on the *Primrose Beach Bulletin* sitting on the rack by the counter.

"Infant Found Being Put Up For Adoption"

. . .

As Noah read the first few sentences, he started to break a sweat. It was Mrs. Tanner's baby. The foster family was giving her back to Child Protective Services, who were putting the baby up for adoption. The stakes of bringing Mrs. Tanner back just went up. It might have looked like she abandoned the baby, so the adoption might not be challenged. Noah showed Dani, who let out a heavy sigh.

"Where are we going to get the lavender," asked Dani.

"How about that candle store by the Italian restaurant?" responded Noah.

They headed across the street; the store was only about a half-block down. Entering the store, Noah's nostrils were filled with a myriad of scents. It was as if he had walked into several different places. There were cedar, pine, and other earthy aromas like he fell into a woodsy forest, then the smell of an ocean breeze, followed by the peppermint scent coming off the seasonal candles on a table labeled "Half Off!" It wasn't long before they found a table of essential oils. They found a highly concentrated bottle of lavender that was supposed to be used for diffusers. An oil diffuser breaks essential oils down into smaller molecules, dispersing them into the air for a pleasant or calming effect.

"What now?" said Dani as they left the store with their purchase.

"Why don't we ask Mrs. Heks for the fourth ingredient?" said Noah.

"And that won't make her suspicious?"

"I have to tell her I borrowed the potion vial. We're running out of time; you saw the newspaper article. If that weed is dangerous, I have a feeling she has it. She is always outside picking up earthly things, like her disgusting beetles." answered Noah.

"It's a long shot, but you're right. I just hope we don't anger her, and she turns us into frogs or some other slimy creature."

CHAPTER
TWENTY-ONE

MRS. TANNER

T he kids texted their parents to let them know they were downtown grabbing a snack after school. Dani watched as Noah devoured the pre-made ham and cheese sandwich he purchased at the supermarket while they walked to the bookstore. She didn't understand where all his food went and was a little jealous of his high metabolism, especially when all she had in her hand was an apple. She was only in shape because she made a point of eating healthy and not drinking sugary soda. Dani was convinced the nearly

100% surge in diabetes over the last decade or so in people under twenty was because of those addictive colas.

Barton's Books came into view mostly because Dani recognized the overgrown ivy. She noticed the green climbers nearly blocking the door handle as they approached the door. The winter rains were only accelerating their growth. Spider webs were even starting to fill the gaps of space where the heart-shaped foliage had missed. It made for a very spooky entrance, and she briefly thought about asking Mrs. Heks if she could help her clean up the door, but then she gave it a second thought. Maybe it would ward off customers, which was probably a good thing, given how dangerous the books were. The door creaked open, and Dani noticed Mrs. Heks on a step stool dusting the bookshelves.

"I'll be right with you, children; help yourself to some fresh tea I just made," Mrs. Heks hadn't even turned around to see who had entered her store, yet she knew.

"Thank you, Mrs. H," replied Noah.

Dani smacked him on the arm. "Mrs. H?" she whispered in a disapproving tone. Noah shrugged his shoulders.

Noah removed the chili pepper, cinnamon stick, and lavender oil from his backpack and set them on the counter outside the office. Dani quietly said a quick prayer, hoping for a good outcome, and decided it was time to come clean.

"Mrs. Heks, do you know what Jimson weed is?" asked Dani.

Mrs. Heks immediately stopped working and slowly descended from her tiny ladder. She shuffled her way over to the kids and came up right behind them, uncomfortably close. They could barely turn around without touching the woman's robe. As they did, Noah gasped. Dani was better at containing her emotions and noticed three new warts on her right cheek. Two of the bumps were growing on top of a third large one. The bottom wart was as big as a brussels sprout, only dark purple. Noah was right; every book trip was changing the witch's face. Mrs. Heks stared directly into Dani's eyes.

"Do you mean the devil's trumpet, Child?"

"I ... I ... am not sure," Dani tried to squirm away to get at least a few more inches from the woman's face.

"In some circles, it's called thornapple; in my circle, it's called devil's trumpet. Why do you ask, and what are these things here?" she moved behind the counter.

Noah pulled the vial from his pocket and placed it beside the other items. Mrs. Heks' warts started to glow a burnt red, but she didn't move or say anything. Dani felt like 10 minutes passed before the enchantress picked up the vial.

"This vial has been in my family for generations," Mrs. Heks murmured.

"I am so sorry, ma'am, it seemed to be—"

"No need; I understand why you did what you did; it doesn't make it right." Mrs. Heks interrupted Noah. "We can try what you seek, but I can't guarantee anything will work. While I have the weed you seek in my office, you know there are more than 50,000 varieties of chili peppers."

Noah and Dani looked at each other, defeated, realizing their short-sightedness.

Mrs. Heks entered the office to gather a few items to make the potion. When she returned, she asked the kids to put on surgical gloves. She instructed Noah to open the pepper and remove only six seeds. She then asked him to place them on the counter in a small wooden bowl. Mrs. Heks brought over a small planter. Growing in it was the strangest looking plant. It had green leaves and brown egg-shaped bulbs about two inches in diameter. Each bulb was covered in sharp spines, like a tiny porcupine. One bulb was open. Inside were four different chambers, each filled with black seeds. It looked like it came from another planet.

Mrs. Heks didn't even ask for the lab information on the exact amount of each item to put in the bowl. She added the ingredients by memory like an experienced chef does with his famous dishes. She muddled the mixture in the bowl with a wooden blunt tool and then lit a candle that gave off a horrific scent. She closed her eyes and started muttering some words Dani could not understand. She had heard foreign languages before, but this sounded like a language with extremely long words. One word was at least 20 syllables long. The witch lifted the candle and let one drop of its melted wax fall into the wooden bowl. As it hit the oily mixture, it started bubbling until the bubbles broke over the bowl's edges. The final bubble burst with such force that it blew out the candle above it, filling the room with a rotten odor.

"Your Chrono Amethyst is ready," said Mrs. Heks.

"Thank you, ma'am. Can we help Mrs. Tanner now?" asked Noah.

Mrs. Heks didn't respond but moved to the office and gathered the silver sprinkles that were now needed with the new elixir. Dani and Noah followed and kneeled next to Mrs. Tanner's still body.

"Which one of you is going in?" asked Mrs. Heks.

Noah and Dani looked at each other, surprised by her question.

"You didn't say anything about that," exclaimed Noah, "besides, you said the book was damaged!"

"You didn't ask, Child. The damage won't allow her to come out on her own, but with your help, she can be pulled out," responded Mrs. Heks.

"Then why didn't you just do that yourself months ago?" asked Dani.

"Sorry, only a book traveler can do this; I have never

been inside a book." Mrs. Heks smiled as if she was enjoying making the kids squirm.

"I'll go," said Dani.

"No, there has to be another way. What if you get stuck too?" begged Noah.

The three were silent, hoping someone had a better idea, but it just became uncomfortable for Dani, who didn't want to lose the courage she had somehow mustered.

"What do I need to do?" asked Dani.

"We don't know where the woman was reading, so we just have to pick a spot in the book that you can start reading from. Give me your finger, Child."

Dani watched as Mrs. Heks pulled out a dagger she had never seen before with a six-inch curved blade and a hilt wrapped in weathered black leather with a large purple gemstone at the end. She started sweating as the witch made a small slit in Mrs. Tanner's finger and then did the same on Dani's finger. As the blood slowly oozed out, Dani immediately worried if the ancient-looking blade was clean.

The elixir was applied to their fingers, followed by a sprinkling of fine silver dust. Dani remembered the sensation she had felt before, and it gave her hope that their cooked-up potion would work. Mrs. Heks handed Dani a white leather-covered book titled *Diary of an EMT*.

"What's EMT?" asked Noah.

"Emergency Medical Technician," responded Dani.

As she opened the book, she noticed some of the torn pages and turned to a chapter that looked unharmed. She was about to start reading when Mrs. Heks put her bony finger to her lips.

"Once you find her, you must touch her and say the magic word to return."

Dani was getting impatient that she almost jumped into the book before Mrs. Heks gave her the full instructions. "Okay, what's the word?"

"*Possnoweegonrelmuski*," whispered the old lady.

Dani sighed heavily and repeated the ridiculously long word in her head, trying to commit it to memory. She repeated the word a few times out loud and waited for the witch's reaction. Mrs. Heks nodded with a peculiar smile. As she read aloud from the chapter, her body began to tingle. Dani didn't really hear the rest since her mind was preoccupied with trying to remember the magic word. The chant was getting fainter. Then, it all went silent.

As her vision cleared, she realized she was in an emergency room. The staff was frantically moving around the floor to aid the injured patients. In the corner of the waiting room, to her surprise, was a purple and silver phantom with its head down, looking defeated. Dani moved to the superbeing slowly with her new technician body so she wouldn't startle the creature.

"Mrs. Tanner?" Dani asked calmly.

The phantom looked up, surprised that someone could see it, and smiled at Dani. Dani moved closer and touched the phantom's ghostly claws while reciting the magic word. Unfortunately, *nothing happened.*

TO BE CONTINUED ...

PLEASE LEAVE A REVIEW AND/OR A RATING

If you enjoyed this book, it would be tremendously helpful to me if you were able to leave a review or, at the very least, a star rating on Amazon or wherever you picked up this book. **Star Ratings and Reviews help me gain visibility**, and they can bring my books to the attention of other interested readers. Thank you!

To leave a review/rating on Amazon, click the link below for e-books or scan the QR code if this is a print version.

https://amzn.to/3uRlYxc

Printed Versions

A Message from J.W. Jarvis

Building a relationship with my readers is the very best thing about writing. **Join my VIP Reader Club** for exclusive information on new books and discounts. If you haven't read Book 1, The Phantom Firefighter, you can download it for **FREE** below.

Just visit
https://BookHip.com/DTHFNNR
or scan the QR code below with your phone

ABOUT THE AUTHOR

J.W. Jarvis lives in sunny California but is originally from the suburbs of the Windy City. When he's not thinking of ways to create inspiring characters for young minds, you can find him reading, golfing, traveling, or just sipping a hot vanilla latte. Visit J.W. Jarvis at www.authorjwjarvis.com

facebook.com/authorjwjarvis
x.com/authorjwjarvis
instagram.com/authorjwjarvis